MY
BEST FRIEND
IS EXTINCT

MY
BEST FRIEND
IS EXTINCT

Rebecca Wood Barrett

illustrated by Cornelia Li

ORCA BOOK PUBLISHERS

Text copyright © Rebecca Wood Barrett 2021
Illustrations copyright © Cornelia Li 2021

Published in Canada and the United States in 2021 by Orca Book Publishers.
orcabook.com

Library and Archives Canada Cataloguing in Publication
Title: My best friend is extinct / Rebecca Wood Barrett; illustrated by Corneila Li.
Names: Wood Barrett, Rebecca, author. | Li, Cornelia, illustrator.
Identifiers: Canadiana (print) 20200272063 | Canadiana (EBOOK) 20200272071 |
ISBN 9781459824423 (softcover) | ISBN 9781459824430 (PDF) |
ISBN 9781459824447 (EPUB)
Classification: LCC PS8645.06366 M92 2021 | DDC jc813/.6—DC23

Library of Congress Control Number: 2020939260

Summary: Ten-year-old Henry discovers a strange, wounded creature
in the snow tunnels of his ski resort town.

Orca Book Publishers is committed to reducing the consumption
of nonrenewable resources in the making of our books. We make
every effort to use materials that support a sustainable future.

Orca Book Publishers gratefully acknowledges the support for its publishing
programs provided by the following agencies: the Government of Canada, the
Canada Council for the Arts and the Province of British Columbia through the BC
Arts Council and the Book Publishing Tax Credit.

Edited by Tanya Trafford
Cover design by Rachel Page and Cornelia Li
Cover and interior artwork by Cornelia Li
Author photo by Joern Rohde

Printed and bound in Canada.

24 23 22 21 • 1 2 3 4

For Oliver and Sarah,
always ready for an adventure.

ONE

Hundreds of icy missiles buzzed overhead. I was stuck in the middle. *Pow, pow, pow!* The snowballs pelted my back and legs, stinging like crazy. Just when I thought it couldn't get any worse—*thwack!* One smacked me right in the ear.

"Head shot! A thousand points!" shouted Jackson in his scratchy voice.

I dropped to my knees and hunched over. A cold slug of ice slid down my neck.

Snowballs thumped all around me in the thin layer of snow. With soggy grenades flying in all directions, I didn't dare look up.

The school's intercom crackled, and Principal Kirkland's voice boomed across the field. "Students are reminded that throwing snowballs is strictly forbidden. Enjoy the snow!"

For a heartbeat the snowballs stopped. I had a quick look around. Over by the forest, Jackson and Mattie froze mid-scoop. Their friends paused too. On the opposite side of the schoolyard, near the fence, was another pack of kids, holding their snowballs in the air. I could see Koko and Lucas rolling a huge snowball up to them. What were they doing? Making a snowman? Didn't they realize we were in the middle of a full-scale battle?

"We're not throwing *snow*balls!" yelled Jackson at the school. He was always hoarse, like he'd been

cheering at a championship hockey game the night before. "We're throwing *ice*balls!"

I ducked my head as a battery of snowballs winged into the sky. *Whack, whack, whack!* Three of them nailed me in the back. I had to get out of here. I started to crawl on hands and knees toward Lucas and Koko. They were the only ones definitely not attacking me.

Bam! It seemed my backside was an especially popular target. Then I caught one across the top of my head. My toque went flying. That was it. I was done. I spread out on the ground, closed my eyes and covered my head with my arms as best I could.

Suddenly someone grabbed my hands. I kept my eyes closed, too terrified to open them or try to fight back. They started dragging me across the snow. I felt my pants sliding down, the snow scraping my bare belly like burning hot coals. I was sure that any second now they'd slide all the way down, and then I would die of fatal embarrassment.

They stopped. Rolled me over. A purple toque with two big brown eyes peered down.

"Henry, are you okay?" It was Koko.

I blinked.

Lucas leaned over me too, grinning. "Man, you got pasted out there!" With his pointy nose, huge

front teeth and giant smile, he kind of reminded me of a cheerful beaver. He handed me my toque and I stuffed it back over my head and ears. "Keep your head down," he warned.

I sat up and realized the mini ice bombs weren't hammering us anymore. That was because we were hidden behind the big snowball. Koko and Lucas weren't making a snowman. They were building a snow fort.

What I didn't know yet was that eventually it would become a *gigantic* snow fort. And that someday it would protect us from things much worse than iceballs.

We were all wet and red-faced, and the classroom windows were steaming up. Our teacher, Mrs. Zink, made us go sit on the carpet on the colored squares. I avoided sitting near Jackson and Mattie and found a spot next to Koko.

We were too old for the carpet. That was for the kindies. But there we were. All my thoughts were being sucked down to my butt, and the only thing I could think about was how much it hurt. I leaned from one cheek to the other, trying to relieve the pain.

"Henry, stop leaning on Koko," said Mrs. Zink. "Remember rule number three. Keep your hands to yourself."

"I wasn't touching Koko with my hands," I said.

"It's true," Koko said. "He touched me with his shoulder."

"That's beside the point," said Mrs. Zink. "Koko's not going to be able to concentrate with you shoulder-checking her."

"I don't mind," Koko said. Ever since I moved here in September, Koko is the only one who has always been nice to me.

"Thanks, Koko," I said. "My butt was getting pins and needles from all this carpet time."

She laughed. "You crack me up, Henry."

Mrs. Zink shot me her laser-beam look of fire and said, "Henry. *Do not touch* Koko at all. Perhaps, if you can't sit still, you would rather go to the principal's office?"

Jackson and his friends all said, "Oooooooooooh" and started to snicker. I stared out the window at the chunky snowflakes that were still falling. They made me feel like I was floating, happy and light.

When we lived in Victoria, back on Vancouver Island, it almost *never* snowed. Mom said it was because the ocean created a *temperate* effect. That's why she had to cut the grass in January and why I'd never built a snowman.

Every year, from November through March, I would wake up hoping it had snowed in the night. I'd roll out of bed, hold my breath and creep toward my window. And then…I would see it. Moss green, apple green, grass green, sea green. People talk about getting the blues when they're sad. I got the greens.

But now we live in this mountain town. I wish we'd lived here my whole life. My new home has a forest out the back door, bike trails everywhere and only one big road through the middle of the valley. And a whole lot of snow.

"Yes or no, Henry?" asked Mrs. Zink.

"Yes!" I shouted.

The class laughed. I had no idea what she was talking about.

"Are you sure?"

"No!"

Mrs. Zink looked out the window. She smiled at me like she'd read my mind. "Try to hang in there, Henry. It will be lunchtime before you know it, and then you can go outside again."

"I don't know if I'm going to make it."

Koko giggled.

"I have confidence that you can do it," said Mrs. Zink. "But right now I need you to pay attention."

"Yeah," said Jackson.

I swung to my right.

"Henry!" said Mrs. Zink. "Take a deep breath. Focus. We can do this." She gave me two thumbs up and tipped her head at me, like she was beaming me a secret telepathic message. I had no idea what she was thinking. I nodded as if I had received her signal. Then I took a deep breath and held on to it, hoping the bell would ring before I exploded.

TWO

The snow never stopped. Everyone agreed that it was really weird, even for this town. There were rumors going around the school that a new ice age was coming.

Well, I was ready for it. Mom had given me my own snow shovel for my tenth birthday. It has a telescopic handle so I can shrink it down to stuff it in my backpack. The shovel part is flat and has a square end that's perfect for digging, scraping and leveling. Which was pretty much all we had been doing every recess and lunch break since it started snowing. With this much snow, we could build just about anything.

Having my own shovel was coming in handy, because the school had only seven tiny shovels to be shared between all the grades. And, of course, the big kids always hogged them. I wrote my name in permanent marker on my shovel's aluminum handle. Mrs. Zink said as long as I was really careful and nobody got whacked with it, I could use my own shovel on the playground.

Every morning I made three wishes before I peeked out the blinds. *Let it snow. Let it snow. Let it snow.* When I saw the sky whirling with flakes, I shouted, "Woo-hoo! Mom, it's *still* snowing!"

Within a few days of the first blizzard, Mom quit her job driving the front-end loader at the recycling depot and got a new job as a snowplow driver. I told her I'd heard at school that there might be a new ice age coming. Mom laughed and said she didn't care because it was the best-paying job she'd ever had. "Bring it on!" she added and then gave me a fist bump.

People said they couldn't remember it ever having snowed so much. And the white stuff came down in every form you can imagine. There were even names for all the different kinds. Powder, snizzle and elephant snot. Sometimes the flakes were so small and light they hung in the air like dust.

The snowbanks got higher and higher, until the sidewalks started feeling like corridors in a maze. You had to climb right up on top of the banks to figure out what part of the neighborhood you were in.

There was so much snow at school that everyone had to leave from the second-floor doors until a digger could be brought in to clear a deep trench to the first floor entrance.

In the last three weeks I had helped build one of the two big snow forts on the school grounds. They looked like castles, with high walls and no roof. Our leader was Captain Frances, a girl in seventh grade who loved bossing us around. She was a good leader,

I guess. She had great ideas about how to build the fort and stepped in whenever we started fighting about it. Each of us was given a specific mission. Captain Frances told us that if any one of us failed, the whole fort could be destroyed.

Since I had a shovel, I was known as Lieutenant Digger. My mission was to shovel out the fort whenever the snow built up, which was pretty much all the time. Captain Frances assured me that my mission was critical. She told me *I* was critical. No one had ever told me that before. That I was important. The job was hard, but she believed I could do it. I decided nothing was going to stop me from doing my shoveling duty.

The inside of the fort was as impressive as the outside. There were two rooms with snow benches and snow tables. If the snow was sticky, we made snowballs and stacked them on three hard-packed snow shelves, even though the school had banned us from throwing them. The trouble was, it just kept snowing. We'd fix up the fort and then the next day we'd be up to our knees in a fresh heap of snow. It's hard to defend your castle when you can't find your cannonballs.

The other problem was, the snow was getting so deep that it was hard to see where the entrance was.

Kids kept climbing over the walls and damaging them. One day Captain Frances reassigned me to digging out a tunnel that would run from the inside of the fort to the outside, so our team could have a secret entrance. Since Lucas was the only other guy with a shovel, she asked him to team up with me. In the meantime Captain Frances got all the other kids making more snowballs, building our arsenal. She said she'd heard the kids from the other big fort were planning a raid on us.

We called those guys the Weasels, even though they wanted to be called the Wolves. And they called us the Packrats, even though we wanted to be called the Cougars.

I wasn't too upset about being called a Packrat. I googled packrat images, and even though it sounds like they are nasty rodents, they are actually super cute, with round Mickey Mouse ears, big black eyes, a tiny pink nose and a fluffy tail. If we had to be named after a rat, at least it was one that was kind of cool.

Over the weekend an excavator had finally cleared the school entrance and shoveled all the snow over the edge of the hill that backed onto our fort. The piled snow was way heavier than regular snow, which is probably what had given Captain Frances the idea of a secret tunnel.

Lucas and I came up with a plan of attack and began to shovel. He started inside the fort, and I started at the top of the pile. With a secret tunnel we could escape the fort if we needed to. We'd also have the advantage of chucking snowballs from the top of the playground. But we had to make sure the Weasels didn't find out what we were doing. It was kind of exciting to be sneaky diggers.

But it was a lot of work too. Chipping at the hard-packed snow and scooping it out was exhausting. My head was sweating under my toque and my gloves were soaked through. But I kept at it. This was a serious assignment.

I had dug deep enough to be almost entirely inside the tunnel, when I felt something kick the heel of my boot. "Quit it!" I yelled. There was some laughing outside, and I figured I'd just ignore them, but then someone jumped on my boot. I felt a ping in my ankle. "Eeeowch!"

I backed out of the tunnel. Jackson and Mattie stood there, grinning. I didn't know if they were Weasels, but I knew for sure they weren't Packrats. As I shook out my ankle to make sure it was okay, Jackson kicked the toe of his boot into the pile of snow-ice I had dug out. A sharp hunk flew up and dinged my cheek. "Ow! Stop it!"

"Don't be such a baby. What are you doing anyway?" asked Jackson, kicking the pile again.

"Digging a hole."

Mattie sniggered.

"Digging a *hole*?" said Jackson. "What a dumb idea! What are you going to do with a hole?"

"Bury a bone," I growled. "Stop bothering me." I gave my sore ankle another good shake to loosen it up and climbed back into my tunnel. Behind me I could hear one of them barking like a dog. The other one was howling. Jerks.

The shoveling got harder the farther in I went. As I picked at the snow, splinters of ice flew in every direction. I kept my eyes closed. Once I'd hacked off a pile, I scooped it out between my legs like a hound. "Watch out!" I yelled. I heard a yelp, and then it went quiet. Well, I'd warned them.

I skewered the tunnel wall with my shovel again. I didn't need Jackson and Mattie and their stupid quacking. Now more than ever I knew how important my mission was. We had to keep the fort safe.

I dug and dug, until my arms turned to soggy spaghetti. But suddenly my shovel burst through to the other side.

"Lucas, we did it!" I shouted, banging the icy edges of the opening away. *Phew!* I could barely see in the dim light, but I could smell something strange, like an old wet rug. "Lucas?" I said, a bit confused.

Lucas was panting. Hard.

"Are you all right, buddy?" I asked.

He growled like an animal. I shrieked and scrabbled backward.

Light poured into the tunnel, and I saw a flash of two blue eyes. And white fur. And whiskers. *What was going on?* Who, or *what*, was in the tunnel? Before I could figure it out, a big chunk of snow crunched down on my head. The tunnel was caving in. I scrambled to get out, but I couldn't crawl backward quickly enough. Another pile of snow fell on me.

I tried to shout, but my chest and face were squashed into the tunnel floor. It felt like I was being run over by Mom's snowplow. The air was being pushed out of my lungs. I couldn't breathe. My arms and legs and body were being crushed under a huge weight. All I could see were sparks against dark gray thunderclouds rolling over my head. Then everything went black.

THREE

"Can you tell me your name?" asked a voice.

"Henry Springs," I replied automatically. I opened my eyes, and fireworks exploded. Purple stars burst in every corner. I shut my eyes tight, and the sparks and fireball of pain eased off.

"Do you remember what happened?"

"I was digging a hole."

The voice had a mustache, and that's about all I saw. The Mustache and another person slid me onto a hard board. I opened my eyes a crack. I was covered in a silver blanket like those hot dogs wrapped in tinfoil that Dad used to get when we went to the Saanich Fair.

"Do you remember what happened when you were digging the hole?" asked the other person. She wore a yellow-and-black coat, and her hair was short and spiky. I really wanted to tell them what I'd seen, only I couldn't remember what that was exactly. I kept opening my mouth to speak and then the words were gone.

They lifted me and the board into the air, and I floated over the snowy field. Flying stars whirled around my head, and I shut my eyes again. Then I landed, heard a click and felt straps tying me down. A door thudded shut. We started to move. There was a flash in my brain of snow and ice crashing down on me. A blurry memory of being trapped. I started to gasp for air.

A warm hand pressed against my forehead. "Hey, I'm Bart, a paramedic, and this is Nala. You're going to be fine. But just to be safe, we're taking you to the hospital to get you checked out, okay? The school will call your mom and tell her to meet us there."

"Okay. Good. Mom already knows everybody at the hospital," I said, trying to sound like this was no big deal. It was true that we knew the receptionist and the nurses and the X-ray technicians and the doctors. I was always falling off something—skateboards,

bikes, boulders—or onto something—pavement, pointy sticks, LEGO. I guess you could say gravity was not my friend.

I laughed. Then stopped. My head hurt.

"What's so funny?" asked Bart the Mustache. My eyes were shut, but I could tell he was smiling.

"This time something fell on *me*. Everybody at the hospital's going to think that's so weird," I said and then stopped again. I'd just remembered that I'd never been to this hospital before. All the people we knew were back in Victoria, where we used to live. My stomach flopped over. "I think I'm going to puke," I mumbled.

"Try not to move," said Bart. "I'll roll you over so you can throw up. We need to keep your head and neck still until we can get an X-ray."

As soon as the board—with me strapped to it—was tilted to the side, I barfed.

"Sorry."

"It's okay, buddy," said Bart, tilting the board back to level again. I felt a cloth dabbing my chin. "We all have bad days."

I squeezed my eyes shut to stop any tears from leaking out, but that made my head throb. I needed something to distract me. "Can you turn on the radio?"

"No can do, my man. That would break the rules."

"Why isn't the siren on? This is an ambulance, right?"

"It sure is, and you're doing great. There's no need to rush in this blizzard."

I held my breath, trying not to burst out crying, and then I heard Bart quietly start to hum a tune I remembered from summer camp, "The Other Day I Met a Bear." When he started to sing, I echoed his words softly after each line.

The other day (the other day)
I took a hike (I took a hike)
Out on a trail (out on a trail)
I really like (I really like)
We sang the next lines together.
The other day I took a hike
Out on a trail
I really like.

Bart kept singing. The words weren't the ones I remembered, but it was easy to follow along.

And in the woods (and in the woods)
I saw a Thing (I saw a Thing)
With tons of hair (with tons of hair)
My heart went zing! (my heart went zing!)
And in the woods I saw a Thing
With tons of hair
My heart went zing!

A Thing. With tons of hair. A memory flash. I had seen Some Thing with white fur in the tunnel just before it collapsed. I remembered the blue eyes staring back at me. The growl. It wasn't Lucas, that was for sure. But was my memory real? Had there really been a Thing in the tunnel with me?

"What's that song about anyway?" I asked, trying not to let my voice wobble.

"It's about a mysterious creature living in the woods, and a guy who goes looking for it," Bart replied.

"There's no *actual* mystery creature in the woods though," I said confidently, testing him. I find that when you say something as if you have a strong opinion, even if you don't believe it, grown-ups will often tell you way more than if you asked a simple question.

Bart didn't say anything.

"Do *you* believe there's really a mysterious creature in the woods?" I asked, opening my eyes a crack. All I could see was the shiny white ceiling, blinding light and a bushy, brown mustache. Sparklers spun at the corners of my vision. I closed my eyes again.

"Who knows, Henry? Maybe. Maybe not. But it sure is fun looking for them."

"What? Where?"

"Pretty much everywhere around here. Go for a walk on any trail, and within a few minutes you're more or less in the wilderness."

By the time we arrived at the hospital, the sparks had disappeared, and I was feeling toasty warm in my magical silver hot-dog blanket. As soon as Bart and Nala wheeled me in, I heard a kind voice at my side.

"I'm Dr. Hollingsworth. What's your name?" she said.

"Henry Springs."

"Can you open your eyes for me, Henry?"

"It kind of hurts. I have a headache," I said, opening my eyes a crack. A blurry face framed with cotton-candy hair leaned in. At first I thought I was imagining it, but then I realized that her fluffy hair really was light pink and blue. Dr. Fluff asked me if I remembered what had happened. The real question was, how could I forget?

I told her all about the tunnel collapsing but left out the part about the furry Thing. I wasn't quite ready to share that yet. Then the doctor asked me a whole bunch more questions like was I in any pain, and how many fingers was she holding up? I had to do some wacko things like walking in a straight line with one foot right in front of the other, and touching my finger to my nose. Dr. Fluff also poked me in my back and ribs and neck like I was a voodoo doll.

It wasn't long before I heard heavy boots clumping down the hallway. Mom swung into the room and grabbed my hand. Her toque had chunks of snow stuck to it. A drop of melting snow or a tear hung off the end of her red nose. She wiped it away, and I could see her chin was a bit wobbly too. She leaned in and hugged me.

"Oof," I grunted.

"Sorry," she said, releasing me. "Can you tell me where it hurts?"

"Everywhere from the waist up."

"Oh. That's not good."

"Look on the bright side, Mom. I'm 50 percent perfect."

Dr. Fluff told my mom that the good news was I didn't appear to have any broken bones. "The not-so-great news," she continued, "is that Henry is showing signs of a concussion." She looked back at me and smiled gently. "Headache, blurry vision and nausea. Has he had a concussion before?" she asked.

Mom rubbed the top of my head lightly. "Not that we know of."

"Okay, that's good. For now, it's really important that he rest."

"Define *rest*," said my mom.

"Henry will need to lie down in a dark room to allow his brain and body to rest completely. And you will need to observe him for any worsening symptoms."

"For how long?" my mom asked.

"Three to five days—"

"*What?* He can't sit still for five minutes!"

"I'm sorry, but it's imperative that he rest his brain so it can heal."

The doctor handed Mom a pamphlet about concussions and then left the room.

"What are we going to do with you, Henry?" Mom rubbed her face with both hands. "Asking you to stay in a dark room and not move is like asking you not to breathe for three days. *Impossible.*"

"Everything seems impossible," I said. "Until you do it."

Mom smiled and squeezed my hand. "That's the right attitude! And you may as well start practicing now. Close your eyes. Time to rest."

I did as she said and sank into blackness. Off in the distance floated two blue sparks, winking. I imagined myself moving closer to them until I realized the sparks were two blue eyes blinking at me. I had the strangest feeling that what I was seeing wasn't a memory at all. Somewhere out there in the dark, cold night, that Thing was thinking about me too.

FOUR

After four hundred years they finally let me and my mom leave the hospital. It was probably only about four hours but it felt like forever. When we eventually got home, Mom led me straight to my room, even though it was only six o'clock. Normally, at this time of day, I'd be jumping on the couch and watching TV.

Mom pulled down the covers on my bed. As I tumbled in, I banged my head on the wall.

"Henry! Be careful!" my mom said. Then she quickly added, "Are you okay?"

"I'm fine."

"You have to take it easy on the old noggin, promise?" She tucked me in, lowered the blinds and turned the lights off. There was a *zizzzz* noise in my brain that sounded like a small chainsaw. It got louder if I moved.

"Okay, my sweet boy, try to rest up. Let me know if you need anything," Mom said.

"Wait! Don't go. I don't want to be here in the dark all by myself."

The covers rustled as she climbed in next to me. "You know, the school told me you were digging a tunnel," she said. "And then it collapsed on you. Is that what happened?"

"I was digging, but I don't really remember much else." I thought of those blue eyes staring back at me before everything went dark. The whole event was getting hazier. It was disappearing into a fog, and I didn't want to lose it.

My mom touched my forehead gently. "You're such a smart kid, Henry. You could be an engineer one day, just like your dad. But no more tunnels. For now. Okay?"

"Got it."

She pulled her hand away and sat up.

"Don't leave me," I said.

"I need to get dinner going."

"But I'm bored."

"I'm afraid you just have to lie still and not do anything."

I reached out for her arm and hung on tight. "Tell me a story."

"You know I'm not very good at making things up. I prefer science."

"Just tell me something interesting then."

Mom leaned back and pulled the covers over herself again. "Okay. Well, my boss told me something odd today."

"What?" I asked, opening my eyes. But it was so dark in the room, I couldn't tell the difference between open and shut. Open. Shut. Open. Shut. Nothing.

"He said that this winter is the most extreme he's ever seen. Not normal at all. He said it's almost like the beginning of…an ice age."

"Yeah, remember I told you I heard that at school!"

"Right! Isn't that interesting?"

If an ice age *was* coming, it was going to be the greatest thing that had ever happened to me. Maybe we'd have fresh snow all year long. I could make anything whenever I wanted— snowballs, snowmen and snow angels. I'd build the best snow fort in the

whole world. It would have turrets, two slides and a snowball launcher. My dad was an awesome builder, except he'd made houses. Then one day he didn't feel well, and pretty soon after that he stopped building houses. I don't remember too much because I was only four when he died.

Mom was breathing louder, like waves in the distance. "Mom. Are you falling asleep?"

"No," she said sleepily.

"So what could be causing a new ice age?"

"Who knows? Could be climate change. Or maybe it has something to do with the volcano that blew up in Iceland last summer. I was watching a documentary that said all that ash and gas in the atmosphere could lower the planet's temperature."

"From one volcano?"

"Sure. A single eruption can cause a volcanic winter. If the ash blows high enough, it gets in the upper atmosphere and stops the sun from getting in, and that cools down the average global temperature."

"So what's going to happen?"

"Well, for one thing, it's going to keep snowing. And there could be some unusual events…" My mom went quiet again, then started snoring. I gave her a nudge with my elbow. She snorted. "People at work said they've seen some pretty strange things."

"Like what?" I opened my eyes too wide, and even in the dark, the pain smacked me on the forehead until I shut them again.

"Like piles of snow that seemed to shudder. Huge chunks that separated from the snowbanks and looked like they were running down the road, leaping into the shadows."

"*Really?*"

"Well, that's what they said. And a few days ago when I was out plowing the back roads, I thought I saw something strange."

"What?"

"It was really snowing hard. The ditches were full of cars that had skidded off the road. I didn't get a break all day. As soon as I finished my route, I had to start it over again immediately. I couldn't even stop to go to the toilet, or the town would have come to a complete standstill. In an eight-hour shift, two feet of snow piled up. It was hard to see where the edge of the road ended and the ditch began. Once I plowed too close to the side, and I snapped a signpost in half and sent it flying."

I laughed, picturing all the broken signposts that would reappear in the spring when the snow melted. But laughing made my head feel like it was being squeezed into a too-tight helmet.

"Don't make me laugh," I moaned.

"Is your head still hurting?"

"Not too much," I lied. I wanted to hear the rest of the story.

"I should let you rest."

"No!" I exclaimed. "Please, tell me what you saw." My heart bumped in my chest. Was it possible we had seen the same creature?

Mom snuggled deeper under the blanket. "At first I didn't believe the guys at work had seen anything," she said. "I thought they were playing a joke because I'm new and don't have much experience driving a snowplow. But you know, maybe I really did see something. A white flash. But when I looked again, it was gone."

"Was it big? Like a wolf?" I asked, my eyes whipping open. *Pow!* went the hammer to my head. I shut them again.

"Hard to say. I only saw it out of the corner of my eye."

"Well, did it move like an animal?"

"It was probably just a big chunk of snow flying off the blade of my snowplow."

"But *how* big? Like a rabbit? Like a fox?"

"More like a large dog."

"Where did it go?"

"I don't know, Henry," she said. "I had to keep my eyes on the road so I wouldn't hit any more signposts." She smiled. I realized she had just been entertaining me, making up a story after all.

"Maybe you could take me out with you on your next shift, and I'll watch out for…anything strange."

Mom didn't respond. I opened my eyes, but it was too dark to see if she had fallen asleep again, so I gave her the old elbow.

"No. I don't think so, Henry. You've got to focus on getting better. It would be too much for you."

"You could pick up a night shift, and it'd be dark the whole time. The perfect amount of light for my brain to get used to things again."

"I don't know. What about the lights from oncoming cars? They'd be like ice picks to your head."

"I'll close my eyes. Please, Mom? Just say yes."

"No. Now it's time to rest, Henry."

I slept a lot. For two whole days I did nothing but lie in the dark. It was *so* boring. When I wasn't sleeping, I felt lonely, like an iceberg floating at sea all by itself. There was no one to talk to or even argue with. Mom was using some of the time she'd taken off work to catch up on the environmental course she was doing online. So I didn't see too much of her, except when she brought me snacks and stuff. Sometimes she read stories to me, or we played card games like Go Fish and Crazy Eights. I wished someone from school would come visit, even if it was just for a few minutes. But no one came. Not even Koko or Lucas. I tried to forget I was alone by playing drums on my belly and singing the song Bart the Mustache had taught me in the ambulance.

The only thing that kept me going was thinking about the chunk of flying snow Mom had seen. Maybe it was a creature and maybe I *hadn't* imagined the furry Thing in the tunnel. Maybe it was real. Maybe I could find it and discover what it was.

Whenever Mom came into my room, I bugged her to take me out on the snowplow. I told her I was losing my mind, wondering if the snowy creature actually existed. She always said no.

Then she came into my room one night and told me the best news ever.

"Henry, you're in luck. The snow simply won't quit. I just got called in for a night shift tomorrow. And I can't leave you home alone, so…"

She said that although it was against her better judgment, she would take me out. But only once.

Yes! I was going to ride with her on her next shift. I'd be on the lookout for a white furry creature with blue eyes, running in the snow.

FIVE

Trying to see anything from the cab of the snow-plow was harder than I'd expected. How was I going to spot a white creature against the white road and whitish snowbanks? So much snow had fallen, you could barely see the sides of the road anymore. We inched along, following the tail lights of a pickup truck in front of us. White wisps whirled all around us. I was beginning to think my chances in these conditions were next to impossible.

At least there weren't many cars on the road, so I didn't have to close my eyes too often. But every time a set of headlights approached, Mom would say, "Shut your eyes!" Light would sweep through the cab, and then she'd say, "Okay, you can open them now."

I stared out the side window as hard as I could. But soon my head felt heavy. The cab had warmed up, and the swirls of snow were mesmerizing…

I didn't know how long I had been asleep or why I woke up. Maybe it was the familiar turns in the road that made me think of home, but suddenly I bolted upright. We were driving along our street.

"What time is it?" I asked, my mouth dry from the blast of the heater.

"Four thirty."

"*In the morning?*"

"You got it."

We passed the sign that said *WATER ON ROAD WHEN RAINING*. I thought that was hilarious. What else would be on the road if it was raining? Although, of course, we hadn't seen a drop of rain since the first day it had started snowing. The snowbanks were twice as high as me now, and Mom was making them even bigger. I was just about to compliment her on her work when something caught my eye. I whipped my head around.

"Did you see that?" I yelled.

"What?"

"I saw something move!" I leaned toward the giant side-view mirror. Through the flying flakes I could see a white hump bounding down the street. Then it dove straight into the side wall of the snowbank.

"Stop the plow!" I shouted.

"Henry, I've got a job to do. I'm almost done this last run."

"Hit the brakes! I saw it!"

"Saw what?"

"I don't know, Mom. But I have to find out!" I reached for the door handle.

"No. Absolutely not, Henry."

"But you said you'd seen a creature too! Don't you want to find it?"

"Henry," said my mom, shifting down the gears, "I was just telling you a story. To amuse you."

"But I saw something!" I said. "I know I did."

"No. I'm sorry. There's nothing out there."

Mom's words weighed me down like a cold, wet towel. I gazed into the side-view mirror. As I watched the snowplow's hazard lights flash, my headache kicked into gear, throbbing in time with the beat.

Lying in my dark room on day four was one of the worst times of my life. Even though I was feeling better, I still wasn't allowed outside. And I couldn't stop thinking about the white creature I had seen running down the road. I knew Mom had said she'd just made up a story, but I also knew what I had seen. It was *real*. All I wanted to do was run outside and track it down.

On day five Mom sent me to school. The doctor had said it would be okay for me to go back if I didn't have any more concussion symptoms.

This was when a whole new torture began.

There were all these rules. First, I had to stay super chill. But if you've ever spent more than two seconds in an actual classroom, you will know that super chill is just not realistic.

Second, I wasn't allowed to play outside at recess or lunch.

Third, since my eyes were sensitive to light, Mom made me wear her gold aviator sunglasses, even when I was indoors. I looked ridiculous, but they did keep the headaches away.

During art class, when we were supposed to be working on our favorite-animal drawings, Koko whispered to me, "Hey, Henry, do you know why the tunnel caved in on you?"

"The roof wasn't thick enough?"

Koko filled in a fox's fur with an orange pencil crayon. "No. Jackson and Mattie were jumping on the roof. I yelled at them to stop, but they didn't. They just kept going until it caved in."

"Did they get in trouble?"

"The supervisors didn't see it happen, and I didn't tell anybody. I thought it might make things worse. Anyway, I thought you'd want to know."

"Do you know why they did it?"

"They don't like you."

"Why not?"

"I don't know."

"It's not fair. I didn't do anything to them!" Pain thumped in my head, and I rested my head in my hands.

"Are you okay, Henry?" asked Koko. "Do you want me to get the teacher?"

"No. I'm fine." I closed my eyes and focused on breathing in and out like Mom taught me to do when I get upset.

The bell rang, and we got out our lunches. I lined up the food on my desk. Apple. Celery sticks. Salad wrap with hummus.

Koko stared at the shiny green apple. "I'll trade you a Wagon Wheel for your apple."

"My mom doesn't let me have sugary treats."

"Oh." She seemed disappointed. But then she brightened. "She doesn't have to know about this one!"

"Hmm. Good point." I handed Koko the apple. "Warning—sugary treats make me hyper."

"*More* hyper?"

"I know, right?" I took the wrapper off the Wagon Wheel. The smell of chocolate nearly made me faint. With one small bite I was overcome by marshmallowy-biscuity-chocolatey goodness. "Why? Why have I never had this before?"

Koko crunched on her apple. Smacked her lips. "Can I have your celery too?"

"Sure! But I gotta ask, Koko. What's *wrong* with you?"

She shrugged. "I get tired of Wagon Wheels."

"I hear you. I'm so sick and tired of beans and quinoa."

Koko laughed and grabbed a celery stick.

During the break it was agony watching through the window as the other kids ran around in the snow. While Mrs. Zink ate her pickle and cheese sandwich, I drew a picture of me and the Thing in the tunnel. It had been so dark I hadn't seen much except its general shape. But I knew it had blue eyes. And white fur. Which was hard to draw, since the paper was white too. I drew two blue circles for the eyes and sketched an outline of the animal with black pencil crayon. Next to the Thing I drew my green eyes, and I colored in the rest of the page with black so all you could see of me were my eyes in the dark.

"Wow," said Mrs. Zink. "Is that your favorite animal?"

"No. My favorite animal is the tree frog."

"Oh, so what is this then?"

"I don't know." I didn't want to tell her about the Thing. She might get upset if she knew there was a wild creature roaming near the school playground.

"Well, it's the best use of the black pencil crayon I've seen all year. And the animal's very creative. I've never seen anything like it."

"Me neither."

"What are those green things?"

"Those are my eyes."

"Oh, I'm sorry." Mrs. Zink sat down in a chair beside me. "It must have been really hard spending three days in the dark with a…*strange animal*."

Wha…? Oh, she thought I was doing an artistic impression of my concussion or something. Well, that was probably better than trying to explain the truth. "Yes," I said. "Yes it was."

The one good thing about having been away sick was that Mrs. Zink had moved my desk. I no longer sat next to Jackson and Mattie. Their desks were now right in front of the teacher's. I wondered if Koko had actuallly told her what had happened. Jackson seemed mad at me, but I didn't know if that was just his regular bully stuff or whether he had gotten in trouble.

Just to be sure, I wrote them a note—*I didn't tell on you*—and passed it forward. Jackson read it, then flicked it to Mattie. He scribbled on the note and then crumpled it into a tiny ball before kicking it across the floor.

I unfolded it on my lap. *Prepare for your doom.* My heart started to pound. What did that mean? They'd already crushed me in the tunnel and given me a concussion. What could they do that was worse than that? I shuddered and then crunched the paper back into a ball and popped it into my mouth, to make the words disappear. I chewed the note during math. We were doing word problems, and by the time I figured out how many scarves the giraffe needed to keep his neck warm, I had swallowed the rotten mush in one big gulp.

Outside a couple million snowflakes were swirling from the sky, covering the field and our forts. I couldn't wait until school was over so I could get away from Jackson and Mattie. The second the bell rang, I was going to escape and then check out the half-finished, half-broken tunnel where I'd been squished. Could the Thing be hiding in there right now? I jumped out of my seat and ran to the window.

"Henry! Please sit down," cried Mrs. Zink.

"Do you have any binoculars?" I asked.

Mrs. Zink's mouth made a flat line. "I don't. But I'm curious—why do you need them?"

"I thought I saw something hiding in the snow."

Every kid in the classroom stretched taller to look out the window.

"Where? What was it?" said Koko.

"I don't know. A Thing. I saw it the other night, running down the road."

All the kids started talking at once and straining in their seats to see out the window.

"Class! Class!" Mrs. Zink shouted. "Focus on your math, or you'll all have homework tonight. No talking. Back to your seat, Henry. And please, don't make up any more stories, or you'll have to stay after school and write an essay about why it's important to tell the truth."

A *story*! Did she think I was lying? I walked backward to my seat so I could keep looking out the window. I sat down with a thump, almost missing my chair.

Mrs. Zink turned around to write the next day's activities on the board. Jackson and Mattie swiveled to face me and mouthed *liar* for the whole class to see. I had to prove them wrong. Before I knew what was happening, my feet had me back at the window. I scanned the field and piles of snow. Was that a new dent in the swing-set mound? I couldn't be sure. Tomorrow I would bring binoculars.

A distant barking started up in the background. I focused hard on the fields. *Bark, bark, bark!* The noise wasn't letting up, and I looked over my shoulder to see where it was coming from.

It was Mrs. Zink.

"Henry! Please return to your seat and do not get up again. If you do, you'll be making a trip to the principal's office."

I slinked back to my seat. But soon my butt was aching like crazy from having to sit still for so long. I considered sliding the window open and squeezing through the gap to escape. Freedom!

Instead, I leaned down to scratch my shin and fell off my chair.

"You okay, Henry?" asked Mrs. Zink.

"I think I'm having an allergic attack."

"You are?" she said with alarm. "To what?"

"The classroom."

The kids all cracked up, but I was serious. I couldn't stop fidgeting. It was like I had fire ants crawling all over me. If I didn't get outside and cannonball into a snowbank, I was going to burst.

"Maybe it's because of your injury. Maybe you need a brain break, Henry," said Mrs. Zink. Her voice was kinder now. "Close your eyes. Take some deep breaths. We've only got a few more minutes until school is done for the day."

After a hundred years the bell finally rang. I was first out the door, sprinting out to the field to check the tunnel. I couldn't find the entrance. And then I realized it had been filled in. For safety reasons, I guessed. So the creature couldn't be hiding on the school grounds.

But I had another idea of where I could look.

SIX

I wasn't supposed to play outside yet, but searching for the Thing was more important than following the rules. Besides, my head felt fine.

I grabbed a flashlight, duct tape, a shovel, two granola bars, cheese strings, a mini Kit Kat left over from Halloween, a thermos of soup, my water bottle and a rope my mom used to tie stuff to the roof rack of the car. Then I quickly made a peanut-butter-and-jam sandwich and crammed everything into my backpack. I pulled out my snow gear, including a pair of tinted ski goggles to cut down the brightness of the snow. Mom would be proud that I was being so responsible. I also wrote her a note so she wouldn't worry.

Dear Mom,

I am on an expedishun to explore the local snowbanks. Dont worry I have packed supplies and my head is ok. If I am not home in time for desert send help.

Love, Henry

I was pretty sure the creature wouldn't eat me, but you never know.

I climbed three steps only to slide back down again. I needed an ice ax. A stick would have worked, but the whole world was buried under snow, so finding one would be a challenge. I looked around and spotted one of the bright orange snow markers that showed where the boulders and fire hydrants

Whenever possible, I take the shortcut. They often turn out to be longcuts, but they're usually more exciting. So instead of taking the boring route around our lane, I headed directly for the pyramid of packed ice dumped between houses. Beyond that were a few fir trees, the snowbank and the main road.

and electrical boxes were so the snowplow didn't hit them. I grabbed a marker and yanked it out.

It worked like a charm. I plunged my new fluorescent ice ax into the ice wall and climbed upward. When I got to the top, I threw it down the other side like a spear so I could use it for my return climb.

As I started to slide down the back side of the pyramid, I realized I should have hung on to the ax for a bit longer. I dug in my heels, but that didn't slow me down. I was headed straight for a tree! I braced for impact, but my boots slipped to either side, and I sacked myself on the tree trunk.

To make things worse, the impact caused a slab of snow to fall from the branches above and bomb me with powder. When I could move again, I stood up and shook myself like a dog. Despite the pain, I was grateful I'd hit this tree instead of flying off the cliff.

Fortunately the snow around the tree well had mostly been packed down by the heavy stuff that had been pushed in by the snowplow, so the tree well wasn't too deep. Mom has always warned me about tree wells. If you fall into a big one, it's almost impossible to climb out without help. I pushed off the hard-packed snow at the bottom and rolled out on my side through the fluffier new snow.

I took a few steps around the tree and stood at the edge of the cliff. There was a massive, powdery snowbank at the bottom that ran alongside the street. Now I was sorry I had hit the tree. Not that I'd had a choice. But I should have slid past, flown into the air and landed on that beautiful, thick mattress of snow.

I was about to leap off when I remembered I had a rope in my backpack. A jump would be quicker but climbing down the cliff face—now that would be an adventure! I tied the rope around the now familiar tree trunk and leaned away from it, feeding the rope through my mitts. At the edge of the cliff, I leaned way back and hopped off.

I pushed off the wall of the cliff with my boots three times before I lost my grip on the rope. I plummeted to the bottom and smacked into the snowbank. I lay there for a brief second, and then *whoof*, I somehow fell into it.

I landed on a hard surface. Chunks of hard snow rained down on me, and a fine mist of ice crystals floated in the air. I looked around and realized I was in a carved-out space of some kind. My heart sped up, and my chest tightened with fear. Would it collapse and crush me? I took a deep breath the way Mom told me to when I get nervous. *Breathe in. Breathe out. Breathe in. Breathe out.* My heart slowed down.

The ceiling hadn't collapsed.

I was fine.

The hole above me let in a little light. I made a snowball and tossed it to get a sense of how big this space was. It disappeared in the darkness. I wriggled my backpack off and pulled out my flashlight. When I turned it on, I was amazed to discover I was in a tunnel. This one was much bigger than the tunnel we'd made at school. I could stand up without hitting my head. Stretching out my arms, my fingers just touched the sides. The walls of snow had a blue tinge like the inside of a glacier.

I held out the flashlight and strained to see. My light only shone on the area about twenty steps ahead of me, and beyond that it was dark. Who or what had made this tunnel? There was no way it could have formed naturally. And there was no way I was not going to explore it.

Suddenly I heard a *whoosh*ing noise. And it was getting louder. What if it was the creature swishing along the tunnel, coming to get me? I prepared myself for attack as the sound got closer and closer. And then it was right on top of me! The tunnel shook, and I cowered on the floor. My heart pounded. But the noise passed. It must have been a car. Out on the road. There was no sign of the creature.

That didn't mean it wasn't waiting out there in the dark. But I had to find out. As I inched up the tunnel, I heard nothing but the sound of my breathing and the rustle of my jacket and snow pants. I felt the hair stand up on the back of my neck. Mom always said to pay attention if your spidey senses started tingling. Even though I couldn't see or hear anything, I just knew something was there.

I kept going. Faster. I saw a sudden flash of white fur up ahead. The Thing! I knew it. And it was running away from me! I forgot how terrified I'd felt only minutes before. I started to chase after it.

I followed at full tilt. My breath punched in and out until my lungs felt like they would pop. I was just about to give up when the creature stopped and flopped over. *What?*

Something was clearly wrong with it.

Maybe it was sick or injured. I had to help. Carefully I inched toward it. I could see its belly heaving up and down.

The animal lifted its head and blinked at me. I froze. I had never seen anything like it. Pale blue eyes, the same color as the walls of snow, shone in the light. Covered in thick white fur, the creature had faint gray stripes above its eyes and two triangular ears poking out from the top of its head. It reminded me of a mash-up of a polar bear and something out of Dr. Seuss with its huge oversized paws, long skinny legs and a short snout like a lion's.

Something about those eyes made me unfreeze. I was still a little scared, but I had this urge to stick my hands in the creature's fur and give it a pat. When I got close enough to touch it, I took off my gloves. I reached out to stroke it. Underneath

its fur I could feel a bone poking out. A low growl
rumbled in its throat.

"I won't hurt you," I said.

Suddenly it snapped at me, its teeth scraping
over the back of my hand. I yelped and flew backward, landing on my backpack. I rolled over and sat
up. The creature lowered its head and shut its eyes.
Was it dying? Or maybe it was starving.

"Poor guy," I said in a soft voice. "Are you hungry?"

A threatening growl was the answer. The back of
my hand throbbed. Under the glare of the flashlight,
I could see two long red scrapes.

But I still felt like I needed to help. I opened my
backpack and took out my thermos. I unscrewed
the lid and filled it to the brim with water. Then I

pushed the lid toward the mouth of the creature, until my arm was within snapping distance. Would it chomp my hand again?

I nudged the lid closer. The white head didn't move. I poked the lid again and again, until it was inches from the tip of the animal's black nose. I waited. Nothing happened.

"Here's a little bit of water for you."

A weak growl.

A sniff. White whiskers quivered. A pink tongue slipped out sideways and dipped into the lid, scooping in the water and then sliding back into the creature's mouth. The tongue moved like it had a mind of its own, separate from the animal, which didn't budge or open its eyes. After a minute the tongue had slurped up all the liquid it could reach, and it disappeared back into the mouth.

"More water?" I asked.

The creature gave a huge yawn and said, "Yarp."

I was stunned. *Yarp?* Was that a yawn, or the word *yes*? I reached out hesitantly for the lid and stopped midway. Was this a trick? Would the creature snatch my hand and try to eat me? I could tell it was definitely thirsty. Hungry too, by the looks of it. I leaned in closer. That was when I noticed the bloody, matted wound on its front leg, between its big paw and knee.

I grabbed the lid, filled it and thrust it near the animal's snout. The nose twitched.

"Here you go. More water."

The animal lapped it up, this time with more enthusiasm. Maybe the first drink had brought it back to life. When the water was all gone, I asked, "More water?"

"Yarp."

"Yarp," I said filling the lid again. This time I didn't bother to pull my hand away.

This went on for a while, me filling the lid, the white creature lapping up the water, me offering more and him saying *yarp*. As it lay on its side, I took a closer look and decided it was definitely a male. By the time I ran out of water, he was holding his head up. When he was finished he tilted his head at me.

"It's gone. You drank it all."

He put his head down between his paws and gave his wound a weak lick, then lay still and closed his eyes.

I had no idea what kind of food this guy ate, but luckily I'd come prepared for a major expedition. I hauled out a couple of sticks of string cheese and peeled off the plastic, then ripped the cheese into small hunks. I took one for myself. The rest I plopped in front of his nose.

A whisker twitch. A sniff. His tongue tapped the cheese and then scooped it up into his mouth. He didn't chew much, just snarfed up the chunks in seconds. When he was done he gave a little whine. I poured some soup into the thermos lid, and he slurped that up too. Before long he'd eaten everything I'd brought in my pack. While he was munching, I took a closer look at his wound. There was a dried crust around the edge, a flap of skin missing and some dark holes. They looked like tooth marks.

"This is not good." I pointed at the wound. "We need to clean that and get a bandage on it, or it won't heal. We should go back to my house, and I can wrap it up."

He licked the wound again, then sniffed the air.

"You ate all the food. I'll have to go home to get more."

He looked down the tunnel, his blue eyes opening wide. A whine escaped his lips. He lurched, trying to get to his feet, but his long legs wobbled weakly, and he slumped down again.

I heard a scraping noise like an earthquake rolling toward us. In one last fearful effort, the creature managed to stand and take a step, then fell into my lap.

SEVEN

All around us the floor and walls of the tunnel grumbled with deep vibrations, and the poor creature, still in my lap, quivered with fear.

"Don't worry, that's just a snowplow. They stick to the roads. They can't get us in here." Maybe it was Mom driving by. She'd freak out if she knew I was inside the tunnel, hanging out with a—a *what?* I held on to the creature as tight as I could.

The scraping roar disappeared as quickly as it had approached.

Yarp, as I had come to think of him, continued to shiver. "We need to get you to a comfortable place where you can rest," I told him.

I eased out from underneath him, then picked up all my stuff and shoved it into my backpack. I put on my gloves and then, with every bit of strength I had, lifted Yarp into my arms. His fur tickled my nose, and I breathed in deep. A strong smell of moss and pine needles filled my nostrils.

I staggered three steps and laid him down again. As skinny as he was, he was too heavy to carry. And my head was throbbing.

I had an idea. I took off my jacket and spread it out on the icy floor. "Get on," I said, patting the jacket. Yarp sniffed at it, hesitating. Then he crawled unsteadily onto the makeshift sled and lay down. I pushed my goggles up on my toque and, using a *lot* of the duct tape I'd packed, taped my flashlight to the strap. There! Now I had a headlamp, and my hands were free.

"Hang on," I said. I put my backpack on and then grasped the sleeves of my jacket. I managed to drag Yarp down the tunnel, back the way I'd come. It was tough going, but I had to get him to a place where he could heal safely.

Since it would be impossible to haul Yarp up out of the hole I'd fallen through, I would need to dig my way out of the snowbank from the side, coming out onto the main road. I started attacking the side wall with my shovel. The snow was hard-packed, and I

could chip away just small chunks at a time. Soon I was sweating. Digging an exit was hard work. That got me thinking. How had this tunnel been built, anyway? It seemed to be perfectly formed inside the snowbank that ran alongside the street. We'd had *so* much snow this winter. I figured the snowplows had made the massive snowbanks along the roadways. But *what had made the tunnels inside the snowbanks?* Yarp seemed too small to have done it, although he did have pretty huge claws.

Finally I broke through the wall. I chopped at the hole until it was the size of a basketball. When I began to pull Yarp through the hole, he whined fiercely.

"You can't stay here. Who will look after you?" I wrenched my jacket. He growled. I felt the cut on my hand aching where he had slashed me.

"You can come to my house."

He growled again.

"That's too bad," I said. "You don't have a choice." I snatched up my coat sleeves and with a hefty tug pulled Yarp out of the tunnel. He howled like he was in pain, but I kept dragging him, and soon we were on the main road, just around the corner from my house.

Snow was falling heavily, sticking to my eyelashes and Yarp's fur. I realized I couldn't take the shortcut home, as that would mean pulling him up the cliff.

I needed to tow him down the street. But there was a danger that someone would see us. I hauled Yarp behind me on the main road as fast as I could. Every time we hit a bump, he yelped, "*Yarp!*" At least the road had been plowed recently, and the fresh snow made it easier to drag him along.

I heard a car in the distance. There was nowhere to hide, since we were pressed up against the high walls of the snowbank. I pulled harder and swung around the corner onto the street that led to my house. My lungs were wheezing like broken bagpipes, but I couldn't stop. "*Yarp, yarp!*" he cried. I heard the car's engine coming closer, the sigh of the tires on the soft snow. "*Yarp, yarp, yarp!*"

And then it passed on the main road without spotting us. My legs and arms burned. Yarp had stopped making noise. I dragged him up the hill, turned left onto our dead-end lane and hauled him into our driveway. I collapsed in the snowbank right outside our front door.

Snow landed on my face, and I just lay there a while. I liked the feeling of the cool flakes melting on my skin.

I felt some pressure on my glove. I opened my eyes and saw Yarp's good paw resting there. He was shivering so hard his white fur trembled.

I sat up. My work wasn't done yet. Now I had to hide him—from my mom, the snowplow and our nosy neighbors.

But where? If I put him in my closet, Mom would find him. For one thing, she is wildly allergic to cats and dogs. I didn't know what kind of species Yarp was, but I didn't want to take a chance. He had a thick fur coat. Maybe if I made him a snow cave, he could stay there until his leg healed.

Mom was on the day shift, so I figured I had about an hour before she would be home.

I thought for a minute about where I could build a snow cave. There was a huge pile of snow at the end of our lane that might work. But, I remembered, that's where the snowplow shoved all the snow. And when the pile got too big, they pushed the extra snow over the edge. A snow cave would be destroyed.

I lay back in the huge mound of snow and felt like giving up. There was nowhere to hide Yarp, and he wasn't strong enough to be out in the wild. It seemed hopeless. I rolled over. *Wait.* The huge mound of snow right here was perfect for building a secret snow cave. I could hide Yarp in plain sight.

The pile had built up when Mom shoveled snow from the walkway into the flower bed. And it was in no danger of being smooshed by the snowplow.

I dragged Yarp off the driveway and onto the walkway leading up to our front door.

Then I climbed underneath the fir tree at the front of our tiny yard. Hidden by the low branches, I started digging. Anyone walking by wouldn't be able to see the entrance.

I tried to dig as deep as possible, almost down to the dirt of the garden that right now had just some spiky grasses and bushes. Twigs from the bushes crisscrossed in all directions, and I had to reroute some of them to the side and pack them down with more snow. I figured at least they'd help keep the ceiling of the snow cave from tumbling in on Yarp while he was getting better.

I have no idea how much time passed. I've never been very good at keeping track. But eventually I finished.

When I crawled out to get Yarp, I found him curled up in a ball, covered in snow. He held one of his great paws over his black nose and blue eyes. Perfect camouflage.

"Hey, Yarp," I said. "Check it out. I've built a secret cave for you."

His paw moved to the side, and his eyes opened. It really seemed like he understood me.

I grasped the sleeves of my jacket and pulled him under the fir branches and into the snow cave.

I heard the sound of a car. It got louder and louder, until I heard it stop in our driveway. *Mom!* I heard her climb out and shut the door.

"Henry?" she called. I remembered I'd left my backpack in the snowbank. I glanced at Yarp, holding my finger up to my mouth. "*Shhh.*"

"Henry? I'm home!" Then the *whump* of the front door closing. She'd gone inside.

"That's my mom," I whispered. "She drives a snowplow and makes a lot of the snowbanks around here. Cool, huh? But she's not ready to meet you yet, so you have to be really quiet. Okay?"

I hoped he knew what I was saying or at least understood he'd be safe as long as he kept quiet. He looked like he was drifting off. He seemed to have stopped shivering.

"I'll be back later with some food and a bandage for your leg."

Gentle growling noises were the only reply I got. Yarp was snoring.

EIGHT

"Hey, Mom!" I yelled as I ran past her through the kitchen and into the living room. I vaulted over the end of the couch and landed in a belly flop. My head went *wham, wham, wham*, and I instantly regretted the move.

Mom was washing a pile of dishes. "Henry, where were you?" she asked.

"Sorry, Mom, I was outside playing in the snow," I said, switching on the TV and my video game, trying to act normal. "How was your day?"

Mom sat down next to me on the couch and took a good look at me. "Great, but how is your head?"

"Fine."

"Didn't you hear me calling you?"

"Nope."

She picked up the second game controller. "What are we making?"

"A roller coaster for seven baby jaguars."

"Cool. I saw your note about the expedition. You know you're not supposed to play outside yet. Where were you?" Her avatar started to help my avatar lay down roller-coaster track.

"Oh, you know. Just around. In a tunnel."

"What do you mean, a *tunnel*?"

Had I really said that out loud? I had better watch it.

"Oh, I built one at school with some other kids."

I had to be careful I didn't say anything about Yarp. I pretended I was playing the video game, concentrating on making my avatar run left, then right.

Her avatar stopped. "Henry. That's how you got hurt. I don't want you playing in any tunnels. Okay?"

"Sure, Mom, sorry." Left and right. Left and right.

"I'm serious. No more tunnels." She set the controller down on her lap. "By the way, you left your backpack in the middle of the driveway. I almost ran over it."

"Oops. Sorry."

"I put it in the bathroom to dry out. Try to be more careful with your things, okay?"

Left and right. Left and right. I threw in an up and down for good measure. "Sure."

"So how was school?" She picked up her controller and started to build a curve in the track.

I was relieved she was changing the subject. "Great!" I said.

"Really?" She sounded suspicious or maybe hopeful. I wasn't sure which.

"Yeah, I had such a good day. It was really exciting, and I learned a lot. I started hanging out with this new guy."

Mom stopped playing again.

"Oh, that's nice to hear. What's his name?"

"Yarp."

"Yarp? His name is *Yarp*?"

I paused. She'd caught me out again. I thought fast, remembering the ambulance driver with the big mustache.

"Bart Yarp."

Mom laughed. "Bart Yarp? That's an odd name." She returned to the game.

"That's what I thought."

"What's he like?"

What could I say? Lying wasn't one of my strengths. He had long white fur? Sharp teeth? Great big paws? "He has blue eyes," I blurted. "And he doesn't talk much."

"No?"

"He is a bit whiny."

"Really. About what?" Mom's avatar was busy herding a baby jaguar into the roller-coaster car. It kept jumping out.

"Oh, the usual stuff," I said, trying to shut this down. For once in my life, I managed to keep my mouth zipped. It seemed to work.

At dinner I asked for an extra helping of mac 'n' cheese. Mom's eyes bugged out. I hardly ever ask for seconds. I guess you could say I'm not much of a big eater. But Mom got up and spooned an extra load onto my plate.

"Hey, what happened to your hand?" she asked when she came back to the table.

I stared at the two red streaks where Yarp had slashed me. "Oh, you know."

"No, I don't."

Uh-oh. She looked a bit annoyed. My mind nearly broke into pieces, trying to think of a good way to get injured. "I was playing air guitar at school, and when I did the windmill, I smashed the edge of the whiteboard."

Now Mom looked like she was trying not to laugh. "Oh, Henry. You really need to be more careful. We'll have to clean that properly tonight to make sure it doesn't get infected."

When Mom went into the kitchen to start cleaning up, I ran to the bathroom and grabbed my backpack. I scooped the rest of my dinner into a plastic container from my lunch.

I stashed the container under the table. "All done!" I said, making a big deal about putting my fork and plate in the dishwasher.

"I can't believe you ate that much food," she said. "Who are you, and what have you done with my son?"

I grinned. "It's me, Henry. Don't you recognize me?"

She eyeballed me carefully. "You *look* like my boy. You *sound* like my boy. You just don't *eat* like my boy."

"I know—it's weird. Lately I've been feeling hungry all the time. Can you put an extra sandwich in my lunch tomorrow? Preferably honey and bananas? Please?"

Mom raised one eyebrow. "Can do."

After we'd cleaned up the kitchen and Mom had settled on the couch with a cup of tea and her favorite science show, I grabbed the dinner container and a few other supplies and bolted for the door. "I'm going outside to check on the snow!"

"Don't overdo it. Remember your head," Mom called from the couch. "And no tunnels!"

"You got it, Mom," I said, feeling a bit guilty about fibbing to her.

Yarp was half-asleep when I crawled into the snow cave. I peeled the lid off the plastic container. The cheesy baked smell of mac 'n' cheese wafted up. Yarp's sleepy eyes opened, and he raised his head. I scooped out a blob with my hand and held it out to him. He licked my fingers clean.

Yarp watched curiously as I retrieved an elastic bandage and a spray bottle of all-purpose cleaner from my backpack. I knew I needed to clean Yarp's wound, and the bottle label said the cleaner killed 99 percent of household germs.

With one hand I fed Yarp another blob of pasta. And with the other, I sprayed his cut with the all-purpose cleaner. Yarp howled and jerked away from me, snarling. "Sorry, buddy, I know that hurts." Since his teeth were bared, I plopped the next blob of pasta onto the snow in front of him.

As soon as he dove for a bite, I started wrapping the elastic bandage around his leg. I had to work fast before he bit me. I propped his paw on my knee so I could loop the bandage under his leg. Under, over, under, over.

Yarp was nearly done gobbling, and I hadn't finished yet. I grabbed a hunk of bread and tossed it in front of him. He sniffed, he chomped, he chewed. I wrapped up the bandage and fastened the end with some duct tape.

Yarp swallowed the last of the bread. He stared at me with his blue eyes, then down at his bandage. Then he started to chew on it.

"No!" I reached out and grabbed his leg. He nipped me lightly on the wrist. "Don't bite your bandages. No."

I raced to find more food in my pack. Seaweed snacks. Three rice crackers. A fruit cup. I ripped them out of their packaging and threw the food at him, and he gobbled it all up. It seemed there wasn't anything he wouldn't eat. Before I could stop him, he turned back to his leg, his sharp teeth slicing through the bandage. Soon he was trying to swallow the long strip of bandage, bit by bit by bit.

"No! No!" I snatched the end hanging out of his mouth and pulled. A long, soggy strip emerged from his mouth like a huge worm.

"Ugh. That is so gross."

Yarp let out a huge burp.

"Ugh. See? Now can you just leave it alone?" I picked up the soggy bandage, which had come off completely.

He licked his wound. Coughed.

I figured there was no point in fighting him. Maybe I could try again the next day to wrap his leg, when it wasn't so tender. I set down a bowl and filled it with water. While Yarp drank, I pulled my large hoodie out of my backpack and laid it down.

"You can sleep on this. I need my winter jacket back for school tomorrow." I patted the hoodie, and Yarp blinked. "Come on. You have to move. Do you need some help?" I went to lift him by the middle, and he nipped me on my leg. I leaned back and tugged at my jacket. He didn't move. So I lifted the edges of my jacket into the air until he fell off.

My jacket now had a lot of white fur and some streaks of blood on the inside. At least no one would see them there.

After a minute Yarp stood up and walked creakily toward my hoodie, like an old man. He curled up into a white, puffy ball.

"Goodnight, buddy. Sleep well." I pointed at his injured leg. "We still need to take care of that. I'll be back tomorrow." I watched as Yarp laid his head down between his front legs, closed his eyes and drifted off to sleep.

By the time I got back inside the house, it was bedtime. But I had to get cleaned up. I was in the shower when Mom called through the door, "Make sure you wash those cuts on your hand with soap and water. And put some antibiotic ointment on to help stop any infection. I left it on the counter."

After my shower I squeezed a blob from the little tube on my cuts. It didn't sting at all. I tucked the tube into my backpack.

NINE

I *really* wanted to tell someone about finding Yarp. But I knew grown-ups wouldn't understand. When I got to school, Mrs. Zink told us to choose a partner and go find a spot to sit down and read out loud to each other. Koko had a book in her hand already and was waving it at me.

I grabbed her hand and steered her over to a corner beside the coat racks. "I have something amazing to tell you," I said in a whisper as we sat down.

Koko held up a book on moths. "We're supposed to be reading."

"Sure, sure. But we just have to *look* like we're reading. I'll go first." I plucked the book out of her hands and opened it up.

"This is a wonderful book about moths. The end," I said and then looked right into Koko's eyes. "Koko, did you know there are secret tunnels in the snowbanks?"

Her eyes widened. "What? Which snowbanks?"

"The ones next to the street."

"No."

"Yes. And remember how I told you I saw a Thing? A creature?"

"Yeah…"

"Well, the creatures use the tunnels in the snowbanks to hide and run around in, so we can't see them. Well, at least one of the creatures. I think there must be more, but I haven't seen any yet."

Koko squinted at me. "That sounds like a porky pie."

"What?"

"A porky pie. That's what my nana calls a lie. She's from England. They say a lot of weird things over there."

"Well, I'm not lying. I'll show you the tunnels right now, if you want. Get your jacket on." I stood up, grabbed my jacket from the coat rack and threw it on. I found Koko's and chucked it to her.

"Henry and Koko. What are you doing?" said Mrs. Zink from her desk. "You're supposed to be reading."

Koko froze, her fingers gripping her jacket fiercely. I guess she'd never been told off by a teacher before. Me, I was used to it.

"I have to show Koko something outside," I said, zipping up my jacket.

"It will have to wait until recess. Right now it's reading time. Sit down, Henry."

Darn it. My plan had failed. I joined Koko back in the corner, but I couldn't keep my mind on moths. Probably the most boring subject in the whole world.

After we'd spent ages learning dumb stuff like how the luna moth doesn't have a mouth, the bell finally rang for recess.

I jumped into my boots and grabbed Koko's hand. "Come on!" I jogged to the door, pulling Koko behind me.

"Let me get my boots on, Henry!"

Outside, the snow was swirling around in small tornados across the schoolyard. With shovel in hand, I crossed the playground and the school driveway. Koko followed close behind. When we reached the fence, I tossed my shovel over. I climbed up the fence and then jumped down on the other side, sinking deep into the snow.

A voice startled me. "What are you guys doing?"

I hadn't realized Lucas had followed us.

"Henry says there's a tunnel in the snowbank," said Koko.

I wished she hadn't told him. I'd wanted to keep it a secret.

"What? Let's see!" Lucas climbed up the fence and jumped over too.

"Wait, we're not allowed to go off the school grounds," said Koko. "I don't want to get in trouble."

"It's just for a minute," I said. I began shoveling at the side of the snowbank, trying to dig an entrance to the tunnel I was sure was inside. "C'mon!" The digging was a lot of work, since the sides were hard-packed snow.

Koko shoved the toe of her boot into one of the chain-link gaps and started to climb. A loud whistle shrieked.

We saw Ms. Shear, the yard supervisor, storming toward us. She liked to smack her mitts together on the last four syllables of every sentence. "You're not allowed *off-the-school-grounds*," she said.

Koko hopped down off the fence.

"But Henry was showing us something," said Lucas.

"*I-do-not-care.*"

Lucas and I slowly climbed back over the fence.

"All three of you are going to pay the principal a visit." Ms. Shear had stopped clapping because she had one hand on my shoulder. She marched us

across the school driveway, through the front doors and into the school office. She told us to take a seat on the bench outside Principal Kirkland's office. Then she took my shovel, tossed it into the supply closet and marched out.

We sat on the bench looking at each other. Koko was shaking. "Don't worry, Koko," I said. "I come here all the time. It's no big deal."

"Maybe not for you," Koko replied. "But I've never been in trouble at school before."

"Yeah," said Lucas. "My parents are going to freak out. Thanks a lot, Henry."

Principal Kirkland opened his door. "Come on in."

Koko gasped and burst into tears. We all stood up, walked into his office in single file and then sat down on the small couch.

"So, Henry, what's this all about?"

Why did he assume it was me who was behind this? Well, I guess it was, but geesh.

"I just wanted to show them the snowbank. How big it is," I lied. I hoped Koko and Lucas would back me up. It would get very complicated if I started talking about secret tunnels and strange snow creatures.

"Well, Henry, the rule about not leaving school property is there for a good reason. We are responsible for you while you are at school, and it is our job to keep you safe."

"Yes, Mr. Kirkland. I'm sorry."

"See that it doesn't happen again. Lucas and Koko, do you have anything to add?"

Lucas stared at his shoes and shook his head. Koko let out a sob. I felt horrible. It was my fault they were in trouble.

"Okay. I'm afraid there has to be a consequence to breaking the rules. So you'll all have detention after school tomorrow. And I don't want to see any of you in here again."

"Yes, Mr. Kirkland," the three of us said at the same time. Then we stood up and headed for the door.

"Henry, can you stay behind for a minute?" he asked.

Koko and Lucas didn't even turn to look—they just bolted.

I sat back down on the couch and hunched over.

"Tell me what's really going on, Henry," Mr. Kirkland said.

"You already know."

"Yes. But I feel like there might be more to it." Principal Kirkland is actually pretty cool. He's one of those guys you just know is smart. Not like me.

He looked at me kindly and asked, "What's bothering you, Henry?"

I stared out the window. The snow had turned to hard, icy pellets. There was no way I was going to tell him about the tunnels. If anyone found out about them then they might find out about Yarp. Which reminded me…

"Mr. Kirkland, do you know how to treat an open wound?"

"Oh! Well, I'm not a doctor, Henry, so I'm not sure if I'm the best person to ask. Why, do you have an open wound?"

"No, it's for a friend of mine."

"Your friend should see a doctor, Henry."

"He's an animal."

"Well, then a vet."

I was worried that if anyone found out about Yarp, they would take him away. Lock him up in a zoo. Or do horrible tests on him. Poor guy had already suffered enough. He was my buddy, and I didn't want anything bad to happen to him.

"That's a good idea. Thanks, Mr. Kirkland."

"I hope your dog's feeling better soon."

Yarp was no dog, but I wasn't about to tell Principal Kirkland that.

The bell rang. "Can I go now?"

"Hold on a minute," he said, leaning forward. Our eyes were at the same level. "You understand you can't just go out of school bounds, right?"

"I guess so."

"Imagine if all the kids ran around doing whatever they wanted whenever they felt like it."

"That'd be fun!" I grinned, picturing everybody doing headstands on their desks and eating cupcakes with sprinkles and throwing water balloons filled with grape juice at the whiteboard.

"No, Henry, it would be chaos. No one would learn anything because the teachers would be racing around trying to keep kids safe. My job is to make sure everyone in this school has the opportunity to learn. That's why we have school rules. To keep everybody safe and on the learning track. When there's disruption, learning doesn't happen. Do you understand, Henry?"

"I think so. It's just that sometimes I forget."

"I understand. But maybe try to think twice before you do anything."

"Mr. Kirkland, most of the time I don't even think once before I do things."

He laughed and then gave me a serious nod. "Stay within school bounds while school is in session, okay?"

"Got it." I stood up and then hesitated. "Can I have my shovel back?"

"Yes. Come and get it from me after school. Off you go. And good luck with your dog."

TEN

I tried to get Koko's attention during class, but she ignored my notes, whistles and owl hoots.

"Can you please be quiet, Henry? The lunch break is five minutes away." I loved that Mrs. Zink gave me countdowns. She knew my happiness revolved around recess and lunch breaks.

When the bell rang, all the kids ran outside and dove into the deep snow. They made snow angels and did flips off the forts. Stray snowballs hurtled through the air, even though snowball throwing had been banned. The supervisor had a hard time cracking down on that one, as there were so many flying.

I did a quick scan for Jackson and Mattie. They were nowhere in sight. The Weasel fort was growing. Kids had rolled massive bulging snowballs together to form the walls. A bunch of the younger kids were jamming snow in the cracks to make the thick walls smooth. I hoped Mattie and Jackson were inside the fort, and I hoped they couldn't see me.

The Packrat fort was constructed differently than the one the Weasels had built. The walls were made by stacking smaller snowballs on top of one another. They weren't as strong, but you could fit more kids inside. Ever since I'd had my concussion, tunnels had been banned as well as snowballs.

But with so much deep snow, it was hard to tell if there were any tunnels until you fell into an opening. So the kids built them anyway and formed the entrance holes out of sight.

I wandered over to the front entrance of the Packrat fort. Koko and Lucas were on guard, holding snowballs in each mitt.

"You can't be a Packrat anymore," said Lucas.

"Why?"

"Because you didn't follow the code."

"What code?"

"No lying. No wrecking. No trickery. And no black magic."

"Black magic? I don't even know what that is. How could I break the code for something I don't even know about?"

Koko turned to Lucas with a confused look. "What's black magic?"

"I don't know. It just sounds cool," said Lucas. And then he pointed at me. "Anyhow, you lied to Koko about those tunnels, Henry. That's why you can't be a Packrat anymore."

"What? I wasn't lying! The tunnels are real. And so are the animals!"

"We never saw any tunnels."

"But that's because I didn't have enough time to dig through. Right, Koko?"

She shrugged. "I don't know. I guess."

"They're right beside the road. I'll show them to you."

Koko and Lucas looked at each other.

"Forget it," Lucas said. "You're just trying to get us in trouble again, leading us off the school grounds. That's lying *and* trickery."

"It is not!" I screamed and rushed at the opening of the Packrat fort. Koko stepped back, but Lucas pelted me with a snowball and nailed me right on the forehead. I threw my hands up to protect my face and battled my way into the fort. I felt two more snowballs wallop me on the back.

"Breach! Breach!" yelled Lucas.

Inside, I wiped the stinging snow from my eyes, hoping to see Captain Frances. She'd believe me. There were about eight or nine kids inside the fort. The big kids were building the walls higher while the smaller kids made snowballs in preparation for a full-on snowball war with the Weasels. The ice shelves were crammed with snowballs now, hundreds of them. Everybody stopped what they were doing when they saw me. Lucas, who had followed me into the fort, shrieked some more. "Breach! Liar! Get him!"

In one smooth motion, every kid in the place grabbed two snowballs in their mitts.

They pelted me with the frozen missiles. I fell to my knees and pulled my arms over my head. There was nothing worse than getting smashed in the face with an iceball. The weird thing about snowball fights is that they sound like so much fun. Until you get pasted by an actual snowball. Or a hundred. They just kept coming. Even though I had my thick winter jacket and snow pants on, it felt like I was being punched over and over again. I really hoped all the banging wasn't going to kick-start my concussion headaches again.

An icy blob went down my neck. All I could think about was reaching into my collar and fishing it out. But I didn't dare. Otherwise my face would take a direct hit. Instead I hunkered down. I was a turtle. My shell was thick and hard. This was even worse than the time Mattie and Jackson had jumped on me when I was digging the tunnel. I expected that sort of thing from those guys. But I'd thought Koko and Lucas were my friends. Or, at least, the closest thing I had to friends at my new school. They'd never been mean to me before.

This was so much worse, because I never saw it coming.

Suddenly somebody yelled, "What are you doing? Stop it!"

The snowballs slowed down. *Pif. Paf.* And that was it.

ELEVEN

"Henry's a Packrat, you idiots!" said Captain Frances, waving her arms in frustration. "And nobody's supposed to throw snowballs unless I say, 'Fire!' What were you thinking? Now we have hardly any ammo to protect us against the Weasels!"

The bell rang, and there was a lot of shouting. Boots and knees bumped into me as the other kids ran by. And then everything was quiet. I could hear small pellets of snow making a *siss* noise on my hood. A thump landed next to me. A pat on my back.

"Are you okay, Henry?"

I sat up. Captain Frances grabbed me under the arms and lifted me to my feet. She took off one of her gloves and wiped my cheeks. "What happened?

I leave for five minutes to check the tunnel entrance, and they all go nuts."

"Do you still want me to be a Packrat?"

"Of course. You're the best digger we have."

"But they think I'm a liar."

"Why?"

Before I could remember to keep quiet, I blurted out everything I knew about the secret tunnels and Yarp. Captain Frances's mouth dropped open.

"You don't believe me, do you?"

Captain Frances nodded. "Sure I do. Why not?"

"You don't think it's impossible? The tunnels? The creature?"

She watched my face, thinking it over. "A lot of things are possible. You know, my dad was in a bad accident." A white puff of breath escaped her lips. "The doctors said he'd never ski again."

"Oh. I'm sorry."

"Don't be! We're going to go skiing on Saturday. First time back."

"Really? That's amazing!"

"Yes, and it just goes to show you that anything is possible." Captain Frances gave me a steely look. "But he had to work really hard at it, you know. Doing the impossible isn't easy."

"No, it isn't," I said, thinking of everything that had happened lately. "Promise me you won't tell anyone what I told you, okay?"

Captain Frances suddenly wheeled around. At the top of the hill stood Mrs. Zink, yelling at us to come back inside. "Gotta go, kid," Frances said. "We'll talk later." She jogged off across the field.

I thought of all the kids who'd thrown snowballs at me and called me a liar. A cold, hard lump grew in my throat. My chest hurt as I inhaled the icy air. The last thing I wanted to do was walk into class and see all my enemies staring at me.

Instead of going back inside the school, I turned and started running the other way. Soon Mrs. Zink's voice grew faint. I ran up to the road and tried to kick my way into the snowbank, but it was too hard to do without a shovel. I climbed on top of the snowbank and started to walk home. The bank was surprisingly solid, with only a few inches of soft fresh snow on top. Every time Mom had driven by in her snowplow, she had added another layer of packed snow.

I wanted to tell her about the kids being mean to me, but I decided I couldn't. She was already worried about me, and I didn't need to stress her out with more bad news.

As I got closer to home, I began to look for the spot where I'd fallen off the cliff into the tunnel.

I noticed there was a huge hole on the forest side of the snowbank. I jumped down and found it was big enough for a deer to squeeze through.

I stuck my head through the hole. Inside was the tunnel. There was the truth, right in front of me. I wasn't a liar. And I didn't need to doubt myself. But it still felt terrible to be accused of being something I wasn't.

Outside the tunnel again, I immediately noticed something that made my heart start racing. Paw prints in the fresh snow. Huge ones. Bigger than my own hand with my fingers stretched out. Which meant they couldn't be Yarp's. I moved in for a closer look. There was one big paw pad and four smaller toe pads. What could possibly have made these tracks? Whatever it was, it had stalked into the forest and disappeared. I wanted to follow the tracks, but I needed to check on Yarp. The poor guy had been alone all day.

I wasn't too far from home, so I took my shortcut through the deep snow. I climbed up the

cliff and the pyramid of packed ice and slid down
the other side. When I got into my yard, I crawled
into the snow fort. Yarp lifted his head. His eyes
looked brighter, more lively, than they had the
day before. I lay down next to him and curled up.
He started to make a low rumbling noise. I realized
he was purring, like a very large cat.

I told him all about my morning. About trying
to show Koko the tunnels and going to the principal's office and being called a liar and getting pelted
with snowballs. He was a great listener—he never
interrupted. His triangle ears were turned toward
me the whole time and didn't droop even one bit.

When I was done, I felt a lot better. I tried not to think about the huge paw prints and what could have made them.

A car rolled into the driveway, and I jerked to a sitting position. Mom. She was home! I heard her shut the car door and go into the house. About a minute later she came outside again and started yelling my name. She sounded frantic. When I could tell by her voice that she was far enough away that she couldn't see me crawl out of the snow cave, I climbed out. I jogged around the lane, chasing after her.

"Mom?"

"Henry! Are you okay?"

"Uh-huh."

"Where were you? Why did you leave school? Mrs. Zink called. She said you didn't go back to class after your lunch break."

"I had a headache," I said. *Oh boy.* Now I really was lying. Getting pelted by snowballs had hurt, but it hadn't given me a headache. Maybe if someone called you a liar, you turned into one.

"Is that why you left school?" Mom bent over and looked me in the eyes, searching my face.

"Yes."

"Okay. But you can't just leave school if you don't feel well. You have to let your teacher know.

You know they have a room where you can lie down, and they'll call me to pick you up."

"I forgot. My head was really bothering me."

"Well, I'm glad you're okay. Let's get you inside."

Mom made me lie down on the couch. I closed my eyes even though I wasn't tired. I heard Mom call Mrs. Zink. She said things like "Really" and "I didn't know that" and "I see" in her hard voice, the one she uses when she is tired and annoyed. She ended the call. I lay there thinking about Yarp and how he was doing. He'd be hungry.

I went into the kitchen to grab a banana for him. Mom was filling a pot with water.

"Mrs. Zink said you also had a trip to the principal's office today. Can you tell me about that?" She plopped the pot on the stove.

"I went outside the school grounds."

"Why?" She banged around, washing the dishes, throwing spaghetti into a pot. She tossed spoons and forks and place mats onto the table and then started chopping veggies at top speed, like she was on *Master Chef*.

I wanted to tell her about trying to show Koko the tunnels, but I didn't want her to find out about Yarp.

"The schoolyard was so loud. I just needed some peace and quiet. It was making my brain hurt."

"She said you tried to get a couple of the other kids to go with you too."

"If you already know what happened, why are you asking me?" I couldn't think of a good lie.

"I want to hear your side of the story."

I sat up. "My head's really hurting. Can I go to my room?"

Mom threw a piece of spaghetti against the fridge. It stuck, then the top half drooped off.

"The spaghetti test says the noodles are ready. Do you want a bowl?" she said. "You must be hungry."

"Not really. I'll eat something later." I turned and staggered up the stairs to bed like I had a blinding headache.

It wasn't long before Mom tiptoed into my room. "Henry? Are you asleep?" she whispered.

"No," I whispered back.

"How are you feeling?"

"Head hurts."

"Are you feeling nauseous?"

"No."

"Dizzy?"

"No."

She felt around for my toes and squeezed them. "I'm going to take you to the hospital first thing, and we'll see what the doctor says."

Mom rested her warm palm on my forehead. "I hope your headache goes away. I'll come check on you in a while."

"Thanks, Mom."

She gave me a smile on her way out. I felt really bad about lying to her.

I napped and then read a book about machines for a while, but really, the whole time I was thinking about Yarp.

Eventually Mom came in and kissed me good night. I pretended I was sleeping.

After she went to bed and I could hear her snoring, I snuck down to the living room and googled "how to clean a wound on a dog" on Mom's cell phone. Yarp's wound had already stopped bleeding, so I didn't need to press a cloth on it or bandage it. Once I found out how to clean it, apply antiseptic and an antibiotic ointment, I crept into the bathroom to get supplies. I moved as slowly as possible so I didn't make any noise. The last thing I needed was Mom asking more questions.

TWELVE

I crept out of the bathroom and paused outside Mom's door. She was still snoring softly. I tiptoed downstairs and popped the medical supplies into my backpack. I added a bottle of warm water, a tea towel and a container of leftover spaghetti.

Inside the snow cave I sat down and positioned my headlamp so the light bounced off the white walls. Yarp blinked in the light, lifted his furry white head and crawled a couple of inches toward me. I pulled out the spaghetti container and held up a single string. I was feeling a little hungry myself, so I lowered it into my mouth. I grabbed another one and held it up for Yarp. He sniffed the end and snapped it up from one end to the other.

While he was chomping away at the pasta, I dug out the bottle of warm water from my backpack and dribbled it over his wound. He jerked away and snapped at the bottle, his teeth clacking. At least he didn't bite me again. I could feel the cold snow melting through my pajamas, but I didn't want Yarp to get distracted, so I kept going.

With one hand I held up another spaghetti string. His nose twitched, poked forward. He was staring at the spaghetti as if he could eat it up with his eyes. Then I held the bottle over his paw. He tried to nip it. I whipped the spaghetti back, and it slapped me on the nose.

"No spaghetti," I said. "First I clean your wound."

I peeled the spaghetti string from my face and held it up in the air. He stretched his neck out, lips quivering. At the same time I sprinkled more warm water over his wound. He snatched the end of the spaghetti and pulled backward. I let go, and it winged into his open mouth like a rubber band. He gobbled it down. I fed him this way for a while, Yarp eating spaghetti strings, me cleaning his wound. Once all the water was gone, I shook some antiseptic on top. Luckily it was the non-stinging kind, and he didn't flinch.

By now he had eaten all the spaghetti, and I still had to pat the wound dry and dab on the antibiotic ointment. I would have to use my fingers and actually touch the wound, which still looked pretty gross. There was bare skin where the fur had been ripped off, raw bloody holes and one long gash. Yellow gunk oozed from the biggest holes, and it had a rotten stink. I had to breathe through my mouth not to smell it. At least some of the hard black-and-yellow crust had softened and washed off with the warm water.

I wondered what a vet would do. Pin him down? I had no idea, as the only pet I'd ever had was a mealworm, and Zippy had never needed wound care. What would a nurse do? Or a doctor? I thought of Bart the Mustache, who'd looked after me in the ambulance. He had sung me a song. About a mysterious creature. Maybe Yarp was the undiscovered mystery creature.

I cleared my throat. Hummed a couple notes and then started singing the song, both parts. Yarp cocked his head, and I reached out to pat his wound dry. His gray eyebrows lifted, and he arched his neck to stare at my bare hand and the red scrapes made by his teeth when we'd first met. I held my breath and tried not to think of his sharp teeth sawing into my flesh.

My Yarp's got fur (my Yarp's got fur)
And great blue eyes (and great blue eyes)
He needs my help (he needs my help)
Or else he'll die (or else he'll die)
My Yarp's got fur
And great blue eyes
He needs my help
Or else he'll die.

I worried the song might be a bit depressing, but Yarp looked more relaxed. I unscrewed the cap from the antibiotic cream and squeezed out a long, curly worm of ointment. I scooped it onto my finger and smeared it down the length of his wound. He gave a low moan but did not bite me.

He does not chomp (he does not chomp)
He does not chew (he does not chew)
My fingers off (my fingers off)
'Cause that'd be rude ('cause that'd be rude)
He does not chomp
He does not chew
My fingers off
'Cause that'd be rude.

I patted his paw lightly. "That's it, Yarp. All done."

He sniffed his glistening wound. Gave it a lick. He made a terrible face, stuck out his tongue and started coughing.

"Don't lick! It tastes terrible. I accidentally used it as toothpaste once. Total barf!"

He tried to lick his wound again.

"No licking!"

Yarp rolled over on his side, sighed and stretched out to rest his chin on his great big paws. It wasn't long before his eyelids began to droop, and his black eyelashes fluttered. As he was drifting off, I bent over to get a closer look at one of his paws.

He had five toe pads in a straight line above the wide foot pad. The monster paw prints I had seen at the snowbank only had four toe pads. Whatever that creature was, it was definitely not related to Yarp. And it was much, much bigger. I would have to investigate.

"Good night, Yarp," I said. He was curled up in a ball, fast asleep. I hoped he wouldn't start licking his wound when he woke up.

I went back to the house. As I set my backpack down by the front door, I heard Mom padding down the stairs. My heart went *boing* off my ribs and back again. I ducked into the bathroom and after a second wandered out with a dazed look on my face.

"Henry?" she said softly. "What are you doing down here? It's the middle of the night."

"Mrrbull, cat gang de friend-o."

"What? You're not making any sense. You're sleepwalking, Henry. Back to bed." Mom held me by the shoulders and steered me up the stairs, walking behind me. "Oh, Henry, did you have an accident? Your pajamas are wet."

I bumbled up the stairs, trying not to laugh, and pretended to walk to her room. She steered me to my bedroom. "Take those wet things off, and I'll get you another pair."

I did as she said and, once I was dressed in dry clothes, fell into bed like I was already asleep. The covers ballooned over me, and I curled up like a furry white snowball in a secret snow cave.

THIRTEEN

Morning arrived what seemed like minutes later. Mom rolled into bed with me to give me a python power hug. "How are you feeling?"

"Squeezed."

"Okay, but how's your head? Does it hurt?"

"Not right this minute."

"Good. I'm still taking you to see Dr. Hollingsworth. She wanted you to come in for a checkup."

On the drive there we had to wait at an intersection for a wailing ambulance to crawl past. Everyone was driving at sloth speed, since the snow on the road was so deep. "Oh man, work is going to be fun today," Mom grumbled. I waved at the ambulance, wondering if Bart the Mustache had seen me.

I wanted to tell him there really was a creature in the woods and inside the snowbanks. I was pretty sure that if I told him about Yarp, he'd believe me.

Who *knew* how many strange and undiscovered animals were out there in the wilderness? How did they get there? Did the crazy amount of snow have something to do with it? Was it really the start of a new ice age?

The hospital was full of people cradling their arms like they were holding invisible babies. Some had their eyes closed and teeth clenched. I guessed they'd fallen on the snow and ice. After we waited for about a decade, Dr. Fluff called my name. In her office she checked my eyes and ears and then asked me a bunch of questions. "Is there a certain time you get your headaches, Henry?"

"At lunch, I guess," I said, which was true. After I had successfully stopped a hundred snowballs with my head, it did ache. A bit. I didn't think it was my concussion, but why bother her with all that stuff?

"Even a few hours at school may be too much for you," she said. "I think you should take a few more days off."

"Oh dear. That is going to be a problem," said Mom. The doctor looked at her, surprised. "Have you seen it out there? It's the Snowpocalypse. If I don't get out there with my plow, the whole town's going to shut down."

"I understand. But if Henry's still having symptoms like headaches, he needs to rest. In a dark room, with no screens, no reading and no physical activity. At least until the headaches go away. Then he can try going back to school for a couple of hours."

Mom sighed. She stood up and put her coat on, and I did the same. On the way home Mom didn't say much. I knew she was trying to figure it all out.

"You can still go to work," I offered. "I'll stay home and rest."

"Alone? No, I don't think so."

"Why not? I'll just be lying in a dark room anyway."

She gave me a weird look in the rearview mirror. "I don't know about that. You wouldn't be able to use any screens. You'd have to just rest. It's really important if you're going to get better."

"I can totally handle it."

"Hmm…I'm still not sure."

"You could get me some audiobooks from the library."

"I guess...and I'll check in on you at my lunch break."

Globs of snowflakes splattered on the windshield like eggs. It was hard to see the road, and Mom flicked the windshield wipers on high. They swished back and forth, smearing the view of the white world.

"I'm so sorry this happened to you, Henry."

"I know," I said, feeling guilty that I didn't actually have a headache. In fact, my head hadn't hurt all day. "Don't worry, Mom. Everything's going to be all right." I didn't tell her I couldn't wait to hang out with Yarp all day long, reading my favorite books to him and eating popcorn. And I sure wasn't going to miss getting pulverized with snowballs by the Packrats at recess.

After Mom took off for work, I hopped out of bed and scrounged up some food for Yarp's breakfast. I thought of Mom as I rifled through cupboards and dug deep into the back of the fridge. Part of me wanted to tell her about Yarp because I knew she would like him. But if we weren't able to keep him, who knew where he'd end up? Maybe I would never get to see him again.

Yarp was really glad when I crawled into his snow cave. He was even happier when he realized I'd

brought him food. Mom would have called Yarp an adventurous eater. Not a picky one like me. He ate *anything*. Week-old salami, pickled onions, burnt toast, soggy Corn Pops, raw hot dogs, limp kale, slimy radishes, moldy hunks of cheese, bruised apples, brown bananas, stale crackers. You name it, he ate it. I had to wrestle away the plastic bag I'd carried all the food in or he would have eaten that too!

Luckily Mom didn't notice any of the food going missing. She was too busy working and worrying about me. Every time she plowed our street, she stopped in to check on me. When I heard the plow coming, I had to leave Yarp, race up to my room and pretend to be reading a schoolbook. When she left I went back to entertain or feed Yarp. All the crummy food seemed to do wonders for him though. It wasn't long before I could no longer feel his hip bones or his ribs sticking out from under his fur.

I couldn't quite believe it, but Yarp's wound was healing really well too. After the first time, tending to the cuts had gotten easier because Yarp didn't mind me touching him as long as he was eating. Big scabs formed over the holes and the long gash. And they didn't stink anymore.

What *did* stink were his poops. Holy moly. He did his business in one corner, which made it easier for me to pick them up with a plastic bag. To get rid of them, I snuck down the street to the local park and threw them in the public dog-poop bin so Mom wouldn't find them.

Three days later, I'd read all my books to Yarp. He was clearly feeling a lot better, because when I went for my morning visit, he was limping around inside the snow cave and whining. When he tried to poke his nose out the entrance hole, I had to tell him, "No!"

He backed up into the cave and lay down. He looked over at me as if to say, *Why not?*

"You're not ready yet."

I knew that soon he would be ready, though, and he would want to leave. I wondered if there was any chance Mom would let me adopt him. But then I remembered her allergies. And we'd have to keep him hidden too. I had a feeling Yarp would hate being locked up in the house. He was a wild animal, and our house, even though it was pretty nice, would be like a horrible cage.

For the past three days Mom had been asking constantly about my headaches. I was getting really sick of lying. That was starting to feel worse than if I just went back to school. Maybe it would be better now. Maybe Captain Frances had told the others she believed my story about Yarp and the tunnels, and now they would believe me too. Except there was one problem. I had asked her not to tell anyone.

Later that day when Mom got home from work and asked me how I was feeling, I told her the truth—I was feeling good. I hadn't had any more headaches for a while. She said that it was time to go back to school.

I wondered what the kids would do to me.

FOURTEEN

Mrs. Zink said if I needed a "brain break," I just had to let her know.

"My brain doesn't like to take breaks," I said.

"I mean if you get a headache or feel dizzy," she said, "you need to take a rest from whatever you're doing. You'll let me know, right?"

The kids were all super nice to me too.

"It's great to have you back," said Lucas, punching my arm.

"Yeah!" said Koko, punching me right in the same spot.

After all the Packrats in my class had welcomed me back by punching me in the same spot, my arm felt a little sore.

The morning went by smoothly as we worked on "invention" drawings. I drew a picture of a rocket-propelled snow scooter. I wanted to draw red flames firing out the back, but I'd lost or broken most of my pencil crayons. I went over to Koko's desk.

"Can I borrow your red pencil crayon?"

Koko didn't look up from her drawing of a water bike. "I don't know if I have a red one. Sorry."

I was about to point out that the red one was right there when Mrs. Zink called from across the room. "What do you need, Henry?"

"A red pencil crayon."

"I've got some extras here," said Mrs. Zink. "Come and take one from the jar."

Koko didn't look up when I came back to my desk. By the time I'd finished my snow scooter and filled the rest of the page with flames, it was time for recess.

I figured if I stuck close to Captain Frances, I might have a chance of being a Packrat again. I followed her into the snow fort, but as soon as I was inside, a whole bunch of kids swarmed around us.

"You can't come in here," said Lucas.

"You're not a Packrat anymore," said a younger kid with braces and straight eyebrows that made him look mad. I didn't even know who he was.

Captain Frances stepped into the small circle. "Listen, Henry's a really awesome digger. And the school doesn't have too many shovels to go around. Not to mention, none of the rest of you seem to actually want to dig when I do get my hands on a shovel."

"But he made up all that stuff about the tunnels and animals in the snowbanks," said Lucas.

"I didn't. They're real!"

"We can't trust him to tell the truth," said the kid with the angry eyebrows.

I glanced at Koko.

She took a big breath and said, "We don't know for sure about the tunnels. We got caught by the supervisor before we could see."

"But that's what I mean!" Lucas said to Koko. "Henry was just tricking us to get us in trouble! There are no tunnels, no animals, no nothing!"

Koko looked down at her boots.

"And that's why he's not a Packrat anymore," said Lucas, slapping his mitts together.

"Enough!" said Captain Frances firmly. "I say Henry's a Packrat. And that's the end of it."

"Then I quit the Packrats," said Lucas.

"Me too," said a few other kids.

Captain Frances shook her head in disgust. "Fine. Have it your way." She grabbed me by the elbow. "But if you want to be a Packrat, you have to prove you can work like a packrat!" She started barking orders. "Lucas, Koko, Jaime! Make fifteen snowballs each! *Now!* Ruby, Nishi, fix up the entrance! And the rest of you," she sputtered, "fill the holes in the walls! This fort is a wreck!"

She swung around and hauled me outside the fort, then pulled me behind the highest wall, where no one could see us.

"Okay, I have a plan for you, Henry."

"What kind of plan?" I was a bit worried now.

"How would you like to be a spy? For the Packrats?" she asked.

"But nobody wants me to be a Packrat anymore," I replied.

"That's why this plan is perfect. The Weasels will never suspect a thing."

Now this was sounding good. "What do I have to do?" I asked.

"Go to the Weasels. Tell them you got kicked out of the Packrats. Find out what kind of fort they're building and where the tunnels are." Captain Frances paused and looked around. "Then, when the coast is clear, report back to me."

I really wanted to help Captain Frances. She was the only one who had stood up for me. But going over to the Weasels meant I'd have to join the same gang Jackson and Mattie were in. I was worried I'd get hurt again.

Captain Frances leaned in. "If you can find out what the Weasels are up to, it could make all the difference."

"To what?"

"The war."

"What war?"

"The one between the Weasels and the Packrats. It's coming. They're going to attack our fort and wreck it and bomb us with snowballs. This is a critical mission, Henry. Are you up for it?"

I pictured the Weasels sneaking through their tunnels, surrounding the Packrat fort, bashing through the walls. I saw the Weasels whopping the Packrats with snowballs. A part of me liked that idea. But no, I was a loyal Packrat! I had to accept the mission.

Captain Frances bent over and packed a hard snowball, whapped it from glove to glove and then held it out to me. "Henry, are you prepared to help us defeat the enemy?"

"Yes, ma'am!" I took the snowball. "But why are we at war anyway?" This seemed way more serious than a friendly snowball fight. She picked up another snowball and hung on to it, as if she needed to be armed at all times. "A few years back Spooky and I used to build forts together. After our leader went to high school, Spooky became the new leader. I told him I thought the fort would be better if we stacked medium snowballs for walls and packed snow into the cracks. Then we wouldn't have to have such thick walls. But he just wanted to keep rolling big snowballs together. That's when I left and started up my own unit. Which eventually became the Packrats."

I knew who she meant. Everyone called him Spooky. I didn't know if it was because he was as pale as a ghost or as scary as one or both. I couldn't even tell you what his real name was. He was only in sixth grade, but he looked like a giant, he was so huge. He had a pink scar like a backward C on his cheek. I'd heard that a dog bit him and he bit the dog back. The dog had needed more stitches than Spooky had.

"Oh," I said. "That doesn't seem like a very good reason to be enemies."

"Well, it's too late now," she said and gave me a serious nod. "Good luck, Lieutenant." Captain Frances placed her hand on my shoulder and then ducked around the other side of the fort.

Now what? Was I supposed to just stroll over to the Weasel fort and ask to join in?

Would they even want me? That's when I remembered Captain Frances's words again. *Henry's a really awesome digger.* That gave me courage. And an idea.

I had the one thing the Weasels really needed.

A shovel.

I ran around to the entrance of the Packrat fort and pushed through. Lucas was digging out the bottom of the fort. I grabbed my red shovel out of his hands. "Say goodbye to your best digger!" I called and ran out without looking back. I pictured Lucas and Koko and all the other kids standing there with their mouths hanging open, realizing they'd just made a huge mistake. And Captain Frances with a small smile on her lips, thinking about how we were going to win the war.

Breaking into the Weasel fort was easier than I'd expected. The snow was blowing in gusts, and most of the Weasels were busy in the field, rolling two massive snowballs. I walked through the narrow entrance and into the round center of the fort. I was impressed by how big it was. There was no roof, but the walls were as high as a stop sign. Nobody could see into it.

A tall boy turned around and squinted at me. Spooky. He was the only one there.

"What do you want?" he sneered.

"I'm Henry. And I'm a good digger," I said. "I'm here to join your gang."

"You're a Packrat," he sneered.

"Not anymore. They kicked me out."

"Why?" Spooky crossed his arms and stared at me hard.

I paused. I sure wasn't going to tell him they'd called me a liar. But I had to be convincing. "They think I'm weird," I said.

Spooky's eyebrows arched. "Yeah, well, I think you're weird too. Aren't you the kid that got squashed in the tunnel and had to go to the hospital?"

"It was nothing." I shrugged, as if getting knocked out and taken on an ambulance ride to the hospital was an everyday thing. "Anyhow, *you're* pretty weird yourself. So that makes us even."

Spooky's eyebrows lowered to a frown. "We don't need another Weasel."

"That's too bad," I said, lifting up my red shovel and letting it swing. "Guess I'll go clear some sidewalks for the little kids then. I'd way rather be digging tunnels, but oh well. If you don't need me..."

"Wait." Spooky's eyebrows shot up again. He watched my shovel swinging back and forth like a pendulum on a big clock. Tick tock, tick tock. "Okay, listen. We do need some help connecting our tunnels. No one wants to dig too far. Not after what happened to you."

I jammed my shovel into the snow. "I'm not scared."

"No? Why not?"

"I've been in plenty of tunnels."

Spooky laughed. "Like where?"

"Just show me where you want me to dig."

Spooky led me out to one of the giant snowballs. Hidden below it was an opening large enough for one kid to cram into.

"That's it." He pointed. A bunch of the other kids stopped what they were doing.

"What's that weirdo doing here?" asked Mattie, scowling.

"Finishing the tunnel," said Spooky. "Since none of you have the guts to do it."

"I would if I had a shovel," said Mattie.

Spooky snatched the shovel out of my hands and tossed it to Mattie. He wasn't ready, and the shovel bounced off his shoulder.

"I'm too busy building these snowballs," Mattie said, puffing up his chest. "Maybe later."

Spooky jerked his head toward me. "This guy's ready to dig right now."

"You're not going to make him a Weasel, are you?" asked Mattie. "How do we know he's not a spy?"

Spooky picked up my shovel. "Weasels work. Packrats pack it in." He laughed and threw my shovel down the hole, then looked at me. "You ready to work?"

"Yes."

"Then get to it, Weasel."

I nodded and dove down the hole.

I dug and dug and dug. During recess and lunch and even after school. Once I'd dug a ways in, the tunnel got dark, so I brought my headlamp rig from home. My hands were sore from gripping the shovel, and my back ached from bending over.

I also had to remove the snow that I'd scraped from the tunnel walls out through the tunnel entrance. That slowed me down to snail speed. It would have been a lot quicker if some of the other kids had helped, but they all gave up after the first recess. Still, I knew I had to do a good job. That way the Weasels wouldn't think I was a spy, and I'd also know where the tunnels went so I could report back to Captain Frances. It was a ton of work, but at least no one was bothering me. The only person I talked to at recess and lunch was this kid in third grade with a pom-pom on his toque. Every day he'd run up to me and ask me for a progress report. I'd tell him how far I'd dug and then he'd go play with his friends. One day I tried to talk to him.

"I'm Henry."

"I know," he said.

"What's your name?" I smiled so he wouldn't be afraid of a bigger kid.

"I'm not telling," he said.

"Why not?"

"I'm not supposed to talk to you, except about the tunnels," he said and ran off.

I felt like I was on a solo mission. I wished Spooky would at least come and talk to me to see how I was doing. The only thing that kept me going was thinking about hanging out with Yarp after school.

The problem was, it was getting harder to keep my buddy entertained in the snow cave. He had a lot more energy. While he was eating the meals I brought for him, I had been burying extra snacks in the walls and floor of the snow cave for him to search for. Now, though, instead of being happy just to sniff them out and eat the frozen treats, he wanted to keep on digging. I was afraid that soon he was going to dig his way out or destroy the snow cave.

I'd also noticed that part of the scab on his wound had come off. Underneath was healthy pink skin. And now that he was feeling better, he kept trying to follow me out of the cave. One morning as I left, I grabbed my sled and jammed it in the snow to block the cave entrance.

"When your leg is completely healed, you can come out," I said. He huffed and lay down. I wondered how long it would be before he just pushed the sled out of the way and left.

Every time I came home now, I worried that I'd find the snow cave empty. After school one day

I took the shortcut home, walking on top of the snowbank. I was pretty sure this would be the day I'd find him gone, so I took my time.

I got to the place where I'd seen the paw prints. I jumped down to inspect the hole. The prints were gone now, but I decided to investigate further. Inside the tunnel I got this feeling I was being watched. I lifted my toque above my ears so I could hear better. The tunnel was silent. Not a breath. But the hair suddenly rose on my scalp.

I spun around.

A huge beast with giant fangs was standing right in front of me.

FIFTEEN

The fangs gleamed in the beam of my headlamp. They hung from the upper jaw of the beast like carving knives. He was a catlike creature, like a giant cougar but with black stripes. He was so big he nearly filled the tunnel. *Run*, my mind screamed.

But then my heart told me to try to make friends with it, like I had with Yarp. I reached into my pocket for a granola bar, silently thanking Mom for always stuffing my pockets with food in case of emergencies—although I didn't think she'd ever imagined I'd be facing a mega-kitty crisis.

"I won't hurt you," I said, my voice wavering. I eased the granola bar out of my pocket, unwrapped it and tossed it toward the creature I was already calling "the fanger" in my head. The bar bounced off his nose. He bent down, sniffed the bar and then gulped it down in one bite. Then he snarled and started moving toward me. My heart thumped in my chest. I tried to remember what you were supposed to do if you ran into a cougar in the woods. Every kid who grew up around here learned it. What was it now? Oh yeah. Make yourself big. Shout. *Don't run.*

I threw my hands in the air and shouted, "*Booga, booga, booga!*"

The fanger stopped for a moment, long enough for me to unstrap my shovel from my pack. I backed up slowly, and the fanger padded toward me again, silent as snowfall on its giant cat feet. *Oh!* I realized that the four-pad prints I'd seen in the snow must be his.

The fanger advanced menacingly. I jabbed my shovel at the beast and shrieked the same high note as when I had nutted myself on the tree. "*Ai yi yi yi yiiiii!*" The fanger jerked back, startled. I let out another ear-damaging squeal and charged. The fanger scrambled backward down the tunnel into the darkness.

Was the scary striped savage gone? I could hear nothing but my own panting. I leapt out of the tunnel, climbed over the snowbank and ran all the way home along the street.

Once there I collapsed inside the snow cave with Yarp, completely puffed out. He gave me a lick and curled up behind me. I told him all about the fanger and how it had tried to eat me alive (okay, maybe I exaggerated a bit). Yarp sniffed me and whined, and I wondered if he knew about my close call or if he was just hungry.

I stuck to the longcut coming home from school after that. But I wanted to learn more about the creature I had encountered. The next day at recess I asked Mrs. Zink if I could go to the library instead of outside with the other kids.

"Are you feeling okay, Henry?" she asked.

"Yes, I'm just curious about something. You always said the librarian is our best friend if we want to find out some piece of information."

"That's right, Henry. I'm glad to know you were paying attention. Good luck on your research," she said, throwing on her coat. "I'm the recess supervisor today."

At the library's front desk, there were two other kids talking to Miss Huffman. I shifted from one foot to the other, trying to be patient. Didn't they know my life-or-death research was more important than the next fantasy novel starring rodents? Eventually they wandered off.

"What a nice surprise to see you here, Henry," said Miss Huffman.

I jumped right in with my request. "Have you ever heard of an animal that's the size of a horse but looks like a cougar, except with black stripes, and has two long fangs?" I bared my teeth and dangled my pointer fingers down from my upper lip.

Miss Huffman laughed. "Well, I've never actually seen one, but to me that sounds like a saber-toothed tiger."

"Really? Are they from around here?" I asked, astonished.

"Yes."

"What?! How come nobody ever warned me about them!"

Miss Huffman laughed again. "You don't have to worry, Henry. Saber-toothed tigers died out ten thousand years ago. They're extinct."

She rose from her desk and led me over to the nonfiction shelf. She pulled out a large hardcover book called *Mighty Wonders of the Ice Age*. She flipped through the pages and then stopped and

held out the book for me to see. "Does this look about right?" she asked.

There was a picture of the fanger, with knife-like teeth, striped fur, yellow eyes and a short tail. According to the book, it was called a *Smilodon fatalis*, or saber-toothed cat, even though it wasn't closely related to modern cats at all.

"That's the one." I could barely breathe. I signed out the book, and as soon as the last bell rang, I hoofed it home on the snowy sidewalk. I kept thinking Mrs. Zink was right—librarians really do know everything. The first thing I did when I got home was show Yarp the picture of the fanger. He let out a loud *whuffing* noise. He growled and snapped at the page before jumping to his feet and running to the entrance of the snow cave. He looked back and clacked his teeth.

"Is that what attacked you?" I pointed at his injured paw.

Yarp trotted back to me, snatched the book from me and ate it. At least, he ate the page with the picture of the fanger. He tore it into long strips between his teeth and paws and chewed and swallowed until there were only soggy scraps of paper littering the snow-cave floor.

"No, no, nooo!" I cried, snatching the book from him. "That's a library book! You can't do that, Yarp."

He howled.

"If you sit down and promise you won't eat the book, I'll read some more." I reached out and scratched Yarp's back until he calmed down. I opened the book on my lap. "See here? The book says there were all kinds of megafauna—that means huge animals—in North America. There were mastodons, which were giant mammoths, and the saber-toothed cats, or tigers. That was the fanger I saw."

I turned the page, and there was an animal that looked a lot like Yarp, except it had brown fur. We both sat there staring at the page. Yarp made little clicking noises, and then he went into a motor-like hum.

"That looks like you," I said. "Says here they're called short-faced bears, and their scientific name is *Arctodus simus*. Is that what you are, boy?" I could feel his body vibrating next to me. I read some more, and eventually he closed his eyes and fell asleep.

How was it possible that Yarp and the fangers were alive? The short-faced bear and the saber-toothed cat were supposed to be extinct. According to the book, they died out over ten thousand years ago.

Maybe scientists only *thought* they were extinct and didn't realize a few of them had actually survived in hidden pockets where humans never went. Perhaps there were valleys tucked between our mountain peaks that no one had explored. Or maybe these were modern creatures that had evolved from those early species in these secret places, and no one had discovered or even knew about them.

So was Yarp a short-faced bear? Or was he a new species descended from one of the Ice Age megafauna? One thing I'd noticed in the picture was that the short-faced bear was standing next to a full-grown man. Its back almost reached the top of the man's head. Either Yarp was a different kind of animal, or he wasn't fully grown. Maybe Yarp was a kid, just like me.

SIXTEEN

So now I was digging all the time for the Weasels and secretly giving reports to Captain Frances. She was worried the Weasels might launch an attack on their fort any day. I told her I hadn't heard a thing about a possible war, but it didn't mean they weren't planning something. A part of me felt guilty about spying, especially since it had turned out that Spooky was a pretty good guy. But there didn't seem to be any way out of it now.

One day as I was digging in the tunnel, I rammed my shovel into the ice wall and the tip broke right through. I slashed at the hole and crawled closer. I'd done it! When I poked my head out, I realized I was on the other side of the field.

I jumped up before anyone could see where I'd come from and sprinted across the field.

"It's done!" I cried, bursting into the fort.

All the kids stopped packing and piling snowballs. They seemed confused. I wondered if they might huck them at me.

"I don't believe you," said Jackson.

"Impossible!" added Mattie.

Spooky pushed through the crowd, past Jackson and Mattie. He peered into the tunnel entrance near the fort, hidden by the three huge snowballs.

"Let's check it out," said Spooky, crawling in. And then he was gone.

"Where's the other end?" asked Jackson.

"Way out in the field," I said.

"Let's go!" said Mattie, heading out into the snow toward the tunnel exit.

"No!" I shouted. "If you all run over there, the Packrats will know where the other end is, and they'll be able to use it to sneak up on our fort."

"He's right," said Jackson. "We have to wait."

"What if Spooky gets stuck?" asked Mattie.

Jackson jerked his head toward me. "Then this Packrat's going to be in a lot of trouble."

"I'm a Weasel!" I shouted, but I was starting to worry about Spooky myself. He was a lot bigger than me, and built like a fridge. If he did get stuck, one of us would have to pull him from the front while another person pushed him from behind. If that didn't work, we'd have to dig down from the topside, and the tunnel would be ruined. All my hard work gone.

Everyone was squinting through the falling snow. Suddenly an orange snowsuit rose out of the ground. Spooky's hair and skin were so pale they blended right into the landscape. He walked back toward us, dragging his boots in the deep snow.

When he reached the Weasel fort he was breathing hard and had snow stuck to his sides. "Wasn't sure I was going to make it out of there,"

he said, coughing. His serious look switched to a grin, and he patted me on the back. "That's one awesome tunnel, kid."

I beamed. Everyone started saying things like "cool" and "you rock, Henry!" I think I grew two inches right then and there. Mattie and Jackson were the only ones who didn't say anything, and that was fine by me.

"Where do you want the next one?" I said to Spooky.

"Can you dig a tunnel that goes from our fort to the backside of the Packrat fort?"

"It'll be hard to hide the entrance on the other side," said Mattie.

"What if we dig a tunnel that pops out close to where the playground is?" I said. "The Packrats won't expect that. And it's not far from their fort."

"Great idea," said Spooky. "Because we need to attack them first. With Henry's tunnels, we can catch them by surprise. We'll throw snowballs from two sides, scare them off and steal their fort." He patted me on the back again. "This kid's got brains and muscle."

Spooky was actually only half-right. The Packrats had been stockpiling ammunition, not because they were preparing to attack, but because they thought the Weasels were going to make a move on them. But at least Spooky believed in me.

Spooky pounded his chest. He coughed up a glob of spit, or maybe it was a chunk of melted snow. "Just don't make the next tunnel so tight."

"Sure thing," I said. "But I'm going to need some help. I need someone to haul the snow out of the tunnel as I'm digging. It's way too slow."

"You got it. Jackson, Mattie, you guys are on scoop patrol."

"Aw, do we have to?" whined Jackson, raising his arms and slapping them once against his sides.

"Let's go," I said to Jackson and Mattie, and without waiting for them to follow, I left the fort and dove headfirst into the tunnel I'd spent so long digging.

I crawled about twenty feet in and then started digging out one of the walls in what I hoped was the direction of the playground. Mattie and Jackson were arguing at the entrance about who had to climb in first.

Honestly, the shovel was the best gift I'd ever been given. Spooky was on my side, and the other Weasels were too. I felt like all their encouragement had given me superhuman powers, and I bashed at the snow. I would build this new tunnel in no time. That's when I remembered my deal with Captain Frances, and how I'd promised to tell her where the Weasel tunnels were. A sick feeling filled my stomach. If I did that now, I'd be double-crossing Spooky.

My good mood gone, I tried hard to think of a way out. What if I lied to Captain Frances about where the tunnels were? But sooner or later she'd find out. And then I figured she'd tell Spooky I was a spy. He'd hate that, even if I did give the Packrats misleading information. Unless I went to him first and confessed I was a spy and promised to lie to Captain Frances about the location of the tunnels. What did they call that? A double agent. A double-double-crosser. A traitor times two.

I slumped down in a heap and watched small blasts of air puff from my mouth like tiny explosions. I didn't want to be a traitor. I didn't want to go in two directions at once. If only I could just lie here and freeze solid. Everyone would forget about me until the spring thaw. Maybe they'd forget about the whole thing.

I couldn't see any way to solve my problem. I could hear Mattie and Jackson still fighting outside, trying to push and shove each other into the tunnel. The school bell let out a muffled *braang*. On my hands and knees, I slowly dragged myself out of the tunnel so I'd be the last one on the field. I didn't want to have to talk to anyone on my way back to class, especially Captain Frances.

For the rest of the day I kept my head down. I was afraid one of the Weasels in the class would say something about my digging, or one of the Packrats would ask me where I had been at lunchtime. It was pure torture, trying to hold still and not make a sound. *Quiet as a fanger, quiet as a fanger*, I kept repeating in my head. When the final bell rang, I rushed to get my snow gear on so I could run home.

I dodged all eyes and made a direct line for the door, but Mrs. Zink stepped in front of me.

"Henry."

I stared at my boots.

"Can you look me in the eye, Henry?"

I kept my head down and looked up with my eyes. Stretching my eyeballs that far made my eyebrows hurt, so I lifted my head a little.

Mrs. Zink was smiling. "You had a really good afternoon, Henry."

"I did?"

"You were so focused. And cooperative. You were an excellent student today. Keep up the great work, okay?"

I nodded. My stomach was twisting, and my heart felt like it would explode in a fireball. If this was what being a good student felt like, I wanted nothing to do with it. Keeping quiet just wasn't me. Being a double-crosser wasn't me.

All the other kids were pushing past me now, and I'd lost my chance to run home and avoid talking to anybody.

"Mrs. Zink, can I tidy up the classroom?"

She blinked like she hadn't heard me right. "That would be very helpful, Henry. Thank you."

I picked up all the pencils and stuff off the floor, and then I put all the books in the library corner back on the bookshelf. Normally I couldn't stand cleaning up, but now it gave me a place to hang out while all the other students left. Twenty minutes passed, and the hallways were quiet.

"Thanks, Mrs. Zink," I said, grabbing my bag.

"Thank *you*, Henry. I'm glad you had a good day."

If only she knew. I ducked out of the school and jogged all the way home. Luckily I didn't see a single person.

When I got home the first thing I did was crawl under the branches of the fir tree. My sled had been knocked down from the entrance of the snow cave.

Yarp was gone.

SEVENTEEN

"Yarp!" I called across the driveway into the falling snow. The world was silent. Where could he be? I sprinted to the shortcut, climbed up the pyramid of packed ice and slid down the other side. I missed the tree, saving my nuts, and flew off the cliff and into the snowbank. *Whoof!* I fell through the top of the snowbank and landed inside the tunnel. With a click I lit up my headlamp. Snow crystals floated in the air, but I didn't wait for them to clear. I walked quickly along the tunnel, calling for Yarp. And hoping I wouldn't run into the fanger.

Not far off, I heard a light pattering noise and panting. I froze. Something was running toward me. I wriggled out of my backpack and unstrapped my shovel. I had to get a better weapon. The fanger might not run away this time.

I searched through my pack, trying to find something to throw. Because I'd forgotten to unpack yesterday's lunch, I had a squished brown banana and three food containers, one full of soggy cucumber chunks. Mom hadn't packed a sword, nunchucks, poison darts or anything else helpful. Spare underwear didn't count. I ripped the lids off the containers and prepared to fling them as if they were deadly weapons.

Whatever was making the noise came flying around the corner and slid to a stop.

"*Yarp?*"

My buddy bounded up to me, his tongue hanging out.

"What are you doing here? Why aren't you in the snow cave, resting?" Yarp nudged me with his snout.

"You shouldn't be out here by yourself. It's not safe." Yarp took my glove gently in his teeth and tugged.

"Wrong way, bud, home's in the other direction," I said, dropping the plastic lids. He kept pulling at my hand. "Cut that out, boy! C'mon, it'll be dinner-time soon."

Yarp let go and backed away from me.

"Yarp! Where are you going? There's nothing out there. Home's the other way."

He looked over his shoulder. Something about his expression made me realize home was somewhere else for Yarp. Maybe he even had a whole family there. I felt like someone had smashed my heart with an iceball. It hurt like crazy.

"Are you going home?" I squeaked.

He lowered his head and whined.

"I thought you were going to live with me forever, where it's safe. Where I can protect you." Yarp came closer and grabbed my glove again. He grunted softly as he pulled. "I can't go with you. I live *here*. With my mom." I looked down and saw my squished banana lying in the snow. I picked it up and threw it down the tunnel behind me, in the direction of my house. Yarp pushed past me and snapped it up. Straight down the hatch.

I grabbed some food from my backpack. "There's more where that came from." I shuffled backward toward home, giving him the mushy cucumber piece by piece. Sometimes he could be so gross. But at least he would be home with me for one more night. Maybe I could change his mind about leaving.

After a while Yarp stopped and sat down. He faced the tunnel wall, and I realized we had come to the spot where we had first escaped. It had filled in since then, probably from Mom's own snowplow. He dug with his big front paws and I used my shovel to bust through the wall, and we raced to the house. I still couldn't risk Yarp being seen. I was happy to see his limp was mostly gone though. When we got back I emptied some crackers into his snow cave and promised I'd be back with a big dinner.

"I had an interesting phone call from your school today," said Mom. We were having pizza for dinner.

"Mrs. Zink tells us never to use the word *interesting*," I said, nibbling at a string of cheese hanging off the tip of my slice. "She says it's not specific enough."

Mom set down her pizza and looked at me. I got a little nervous.

"Well, in fact it was Mrs. Zink who called me. She wanted to check in with me, since you've had to deal with such a lot lately. She said you had a great day today. That you were very focused. And you cleaned up the classroom."

"I did," I said, picking a mushroom off my pizza slice.

"But she also said something I thought was a little weird."

Uh-oh. "It's a pretty weird school, Mom. I'm just doing my best to fit in."

Mom took a bite of her pizza and chewed. "I mentioned how nice it was that you'd made one friend. A boy named Bart Yarp."

"Yeah…Bart's awesome. We get along great."

"So you said. But Mrs. Zink couldn't recall anybody by that name at the school."

"Oh," I said in a small voice. "Well, maybe it's a nickname. You wouldn't believe how many kids have nicknames. There's this kid who is really pale and everyone calls him—"

"I'm worried, Henry. Why are you telling stories?"

Not stories. Porky pies. Pure lies, and I felt terrible for doing it. But I had to protect Yarp.

"Are kids being mean to you at school?" Mom was not letting this drop.

"No," I said, taking a huge bite of my pizza.

"Is anyone bullying you?"

I tapped my lips. *Can't talk with my mouth full.*

"You know you can tell me anything, right?"

I nodded and made some *mmm* sounds.

"Do you have friends at school? Real friends?"

Did I? Koko and Lucas were out now. I did have

at least two enemies, Jackson and Mattie, but telling Mom that wouldn't calm her down at all. "Well, there's Spooky and Captain Frances," I said. They were sort-of friends, I guessed.

"Spooky and Captain Frances," said Mom, repeating the names slowly. Her lips pinched together. "Are they real?"

"Oh yeah, they're real. Like I said, lots of kids have weird nicknames. Spooky is the leader of the Weasels, and Captain Frances runs the Packrats."

"What are those?"

"Two teams that play together at recess." I was stretching the truth like pulling taffy, but I didn't want her to freak out even more.

"Well, that sounds like fun." I could see her relaxing a bit. "Which team are you on?"

I picked up our plates and carried them to the sink. "Both."

"Really? How does that work?"

I was so tired of telling fibs and lies. Not only could I not keep them straight, but I just didn't feel like myself. And the worst thing was, coming up with fake answers was even getting a little easier. This wasn't me. I felt bad every time a lie came out of my mouth.

"I'm sort of like a referee."

"That's wonderful, Henry. I bet you're good at that. When you're a ref, you can't take sides."

"Yeah. I'm not too good at that," I said. I guessed technically I wasn't taking sides if I was spying on the Weasels *and* spying on the Packrats.

Mom smiled at me. "But that's a good thing, Henry. As a referee you have to be neutral. You can't be on any one side."

"Oh, I get it." Boy, did I get it. But being a double agent was the opposite of being a referee. I was a double-crosser. I wasn't on anyone's side, which meant no one would be on my side either. And when they found out…I would be enemies with everyone.

Once Mom had gone to bed, I snuck out to give Yarp a couple slices of leftover pizza. He munched them down, mushrooms and all. I felt sad watching him eat, thinking it might be the last time I could do this. I stuck my hand in his neck fur. "I sure like you, Yarp."

"Yarp," he said, yawning.

"Good night." And goodbye, I thought. But I couldn't say it out loud.

I couldn't fall asleep. My mind was whirling. Everything was going wrong. Mom was worried about me. I'd double-crossed Captain Frances and lost my friends Koko and Lucas. Spooky and the Weasels were going to bury me in a snowy grave when they found out the truth—if the rest of the Packrats didn't get to me first. And the worst thing of all, Yarp wanted to leave. Even though school had been terrible lately, I was happy with him around. He listened to all my problems. He made me laugh, and I liked helping him.

I thought about faking a fever in the morning and skipping school to avoid the whole mess. But deep down I knew the problems would still be there the day after that. I had to face them. Sooner rather than later. Tomorrow morning I would sneak out and give Yarp his last breakfast, and we would say goodbye.

Unless…

…I had an idea starting to form…

Unless we didn't.

I sat upright in my bed. What if I went with Yarp? That would solve everything!

EIGHTEEN

I snuck out of bed and packed up all my supplies. Food. Apple juice. A toothbrush. The camping gear was stuffed in a box in the garage. I dug it out and grabbed a sleeping bag, a pillow and the little tent. I also dropped a hammer in my backpack, just in case we ran into the fanger again.

Once I had stacked all the stuff outside the front door, I realized there was no way I could carry it all. I'd have to ditch some of the supplies. But what? I needed everything. I kicked my rolled-up sleeping bag so hard it slammed into my sled, propped up against the house. It crashed to the ground. I held my breath, hoping the noise hadn't woken Mom.

Yarp's head popped out of the snow cave. He grunted and made a few clicks with his tongue. He eyed my mound of gear, snapped up the tent drawstring in his teeth and dragged it over. He was a genius! Together we piled the tent, sleeping bag, my backpack and the food bag onto the sled.

Yarp grunted at me, turned his back and loped off down our driveway. I stared at the rope tied to the end of the sled. All I had to do was pick it up. I'd be free.

"Wait!" I shout-whispered. "I have to leave a note for my mom!" I ran back into the house.

Dear Mom,

I am going away to live with my friend Bart Yarp. It will be a lot easier for you, and you won't have to lisen to things that aren't true. dont worry I have packed lots of good stuff and I have my shovel and a hammer.

Love, Henry

I shut the door quietly. Yarp was waiting for me on the corner. He huffed twice as if to say *Come on*, then turned down the street to the snowbank on the main road. He sniffed along the snowbank until he came to the spot where we'd escaped before. Yarp swiped at the snowbank with his paw and easily broke through where the hole had filled in with snowplow spray and fresh snow. He jumped inside. I hauled the sled over the lip, but my backpack and the tent rolled off into the street.

"Wait!"

Yarp's nose poked out of the hole. "I have to tie all this stuff down."

I put my headlamp on over my toque and used a bunch of string to tie down my gear between the side handles on the sled.

As soon as I'd secured everything, Yarp set off at a gallop. I found it hard to keep up. Eventually we came to a pretty steep downhill section in the tunnel. The sled kept banging into the back of my boots. I was going as fast as I could, but eventually I stopped and crouched to take a breather. That's when I lost my balance and tipped backward onto the sled.

The sled immediately started sliding down the hill, with me flat on my back like a turtle, arms and legs flailing. At each curve the sled slid up the walls of the tunnel, so high it would nearly flip. It was like being on a roller coaster, only without the bar to hold you in. I screamed in terror, sure the sled would crash any second.

Yarp looked back and saw me shooting toward him like a rocket. He tried to run, his furry hind legs pumping up and down. But the sled was gaining. Eventually the front end clipped his heels, and he launched into the air. As the sled continued to speed forward, he landed on top of me with a *whump*.

I couldn't see a thing, just swirling sparkles of light from my headlamp as we sped along. The whole world was spinning faster and faster. Then we hit a sharp corner and swooped high up the wall, across the ceiling of the snowbank tunnel and down the other side. Just when I thought we were doomed, the pitch of the tunnel started to angle uphill. We slithered to a stop.

Yarp crawled off me. He shook himself and wobbled away.

"Hey, wait for me!" I said, gasping for air. I was afraid to lose sight of him, even though there was only one way to go. But my stuff was scattered up and down the tunnel. I raced around snatching things up and anchoring them before chasing after him, tugging the sled behind me.

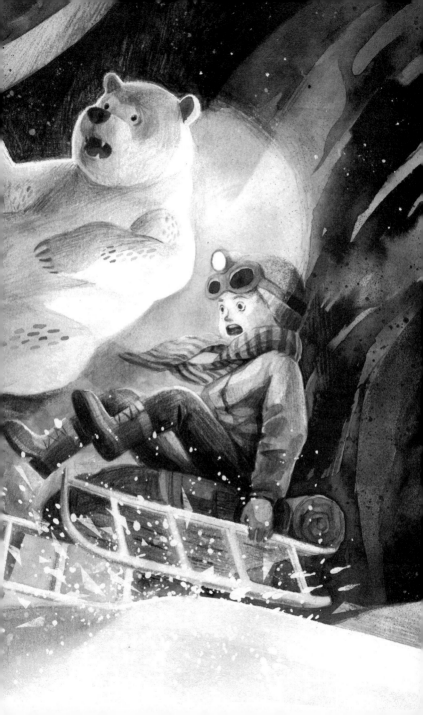

I walked for ages, and my back, legs and arms ached from pulling the sled and from the crazy ride. I stopped for a drink of water from my thermos. I wondered if Yarp was waiting or if he'd abandoned me. Did he know where we were going? And how to get back to his home? Were we still in town or beyond? Had we reached the great stretch of wilderness before the next town?

"Yarp!" I yelled, but there was no sign of him.

I was so tired I lay down and rolled over on my side, panting. I closed my eyes. There was no sound, just the pounding of my heart. If Yarp had left me for good, it was going to take forever to get back home. I started to cry, but I was so tired all I could do was sniff a few times. It was lonely being the only one in a dark snowbank, miles from home and with no friends or my mom to help me.

I began to cry for real. Big gulps, with tears dripping off my chin.

Suddenly I felt a big, wet tongue lick the side of my face. I opened my eyes. Yarp was hanging over me. I'd never been so happy in my life to have a stripe of slobber oozing down my cheek. He nudged me with his nose. I sat up. He kept poking me in the chest.

"What?" I said. "What do you want? Do you want me to go home? We've come all this way."

Poke, poke.

"But I don't want to go home without you."

Shove, shove.

"I know I'm not as fast, but I can do it. Just… wait for me. Please?"

He head-butted me in the belly, and I rolled back onto the sled. It was turtle time.

He butted me again.

"Hey! That wasn't nice!"

I felt the sled jerk forward. Yarp had the sled rope in his teeth and was hauling me through the snowbank tunnel. He was my sled yarp! After a while I turned off my headlamp. There wasn't anything to see except for white walls and Yarp's furry butt. Because of my concussion, I was used to the dark now. The dark was my friend.

Yarp pulled me on the sled through the tunnel for what felt like all night. I was turning into an icicle. My whole body shivered, and my teeth clacked together like I was a nervous skeleton. I couldn't feel my feet or hands, and my eyelashes were crusted with ice. If only I had a thick fur coat like Yarp's to keep me warm. Wherever we were going, I would arrive as one big ice cube.

I had a dream that I was so cold I started to feel warm. My teeth stopped snapping, and I was wrapped in the most delicious heat. Like the time Bart the Mustache rolled me up in that magical hot-dog blanket. An earthy, wet-dog smell filled my nostrils. A hair went up my nose. I sneezed. The warmth around me jumped.

Jumped!

NINETEEN

In the dim gray light all I could see was white fuzz.
Yarp hair, up close. This was no dream. I was lying
on a warm mattress. A living, breathing mattress.
An extra-big Yarp. There was another creature at
my back, and one at my feet—that was at least three
Yarps! Propping myself up on my elbows, I saw I
was surrounded by more than a dozen creatures, all
snoozing. They looked exactly like Yarp, except they
were more than twice his size! The creatures had
short snouts, just like in the pictures of the short-
faced bears in the book about the Ice Age.

Maybe they really were *Arctodus simus,* or,
if naming was up to me, *Yarpie giganticus.*

Yarp—my yarp—was lying at my feet, snoring. He was much smaller than the others, and I realized I'd been right. Yarp was just like me, a kid. Somehow he'd been separated from his family or gotten lost. Then he must have been attacked by a fanger and nearly starved to death. That's when I found him.

Yarp's eyes opened, and he made his low, rumbling purring sound. I could tell he was happy to see me. The eyes of the other yarpies blinked open too, and I could see they were all the same crystal blue. The yarpies started moving— stretching, yawning, scratching. A couple of smaller yarpies crawled out from underneath the bigger ones, bounced over to Yarp and started rolling around with him, play fighting. I guessed they were kids too. One of the big yarpies sniffed my head and neck. Its whiskers tickled like crazy. I couldn't help laughing. Then the yarpie licked my cheek with its giant tongue. Just like my little Yarp. Must be related, I figured. Mom? Dad? Auntie? Big brother? It was hard to tell. His family. I thought of Mom, my only family, and wished she was here too. My heart felt swollen, I missed her so much.

The whole group rose together and crawled to the edge of a hole nearby. One of the bigger yarpies climbed through the hole. A moment passed before his snout appeared again, and he whuffed softly. The others followed. For a second I was worried I wouldn't be able to tell my Yarp apart from the rest, but then I saw the pink strip of skin on his front leg, where he was still missing fur. Plus, he always looked at me like he was excited to see me, like I was going to feed him the best treat ever or play some goofy game. I followed them to the surface, where cold, sharp air hit my face.

We were in a forest. Snow sifted through the pine trees, forming huge white pillows around the trunks.

Now that we were out of the cave, I could see how large the yarpies were. They were also quite thin. It reminded me of how Yarp had looked when I'd first found him. Their furry coats didn't seem to fit right. Were they starving?

One of the yarpies stood at the edge of the group, staring into the forest, while the rest roamed between the trees on trails of packed-down snow. They stopped to nibble at the light green strings that hung from the branches. I remembered Mrs. Zink had told us it was called beard lichen, or old man's beard, and it grew by just one millimeter a year. She said the air had to be really clean for lichen to grow. We were probably really far from the highway.

There were no sounds of cars or people, only the wind sighing in the treetops.

Yarp snatched up a long string of lichen and then bolted off, zipping in between all the yarpies. Two little yarpies chased after him.

Seeing the yarpies eat reminded me I felt hungry, so I returned to the big snow cave where we had slept. The light in the den was dim, but my bright sled stood out against the packed snow of the cave floor. I opened up my backpack and pulled out a bar of fruit leather. Suddenly Yarp was at my side, his tongue hanging out. Some things never changed.

I chewed on the fruit leather slowly. "You've got that green stuff to eat. The lichen."

Yarp smacked his lips.

"I have to make my food last. I can't eat lichen." I didn't actually know if that was true, but it didn't look too appetizing. Maybe lichen was poisonous to humans. Mrs. Zink hadn't covered that in class, probably because we had grocery stores you could stroll into and get any kind of food you wanted.

All of a sudden the forest started to look like a hard place to live in winter. Snow and trees and moss—that's all there was. Maybe leaving home hadn't been such a brilliant idea.

Yarp leaned toward my fruit leather, and I pulled it away. I chewed for a moment and then handed half to Yarp. He gobbled it up in a flash.

Suddenly there was a horrifying scream and then a whirl of shrieks and roars. The fur on Yarp's back stood up, and he scrambled to the opening of the den. He looked back at me, growling, then charged out, teeth snapping. I was right behind him.

TWENTY

The forest was a blur of creatures bouncing off each other like bumper cars. The yarpies ran in all directions, trying to escape the long teeth and enormous claws of the angry fangers. In front of me, a fanger howled at two of the bigger yarpies. They were about the same size, except the fanger had way bigger teeth.

The fanger leaned back on its haunches and leapt at one of the yarpies, knocking him onto his back. The other yarpie, who was the biggest one of them all, swatted the beast with his paw, but the fanger had sunk his teeth into the first yarpie's back leg and wasn't letting go.

Yarp dove at the fanger and nipped his haunches. The fanger booted him in the chest. Yarp howled and flew backward, tumbling into a tree well. I expected him to come bounding out again, but there was no sign of him. My breath came in ragged gasps. Was he okay?

I ran back to the cave and dove in headfirst. My cold fingers struggled to untie the shovel from my backpack. I wrenched it free and grabbed my hammer too, jamming the wide end into my coat pocket before scrambling back out. The yarpies were losing the battle. Many had run off, their blood streaking the snow. The biggest yarpie was lying on the ground, snarling as several fangers circled it slowly. Some of the fangers had bloody bite marks on their shoulders and haunches. One limped badly.

There were four of them, and one of me. But they hadn't noticed me yet. I had to distract them before they finished off the big yarpie. I raised my mighty shovel and screamed a high-pitched *"Ai yi yi yi yiiiii!"* I ran into the circle of fangers. With all the strength my string-bean arms could muster, I smashed one of the beasts on the nose. He yowled and shot off into the woods. I lifted my shovel high above my head. The other three stepped closer. And closer. I could smell their rotten breath. I aimed for an even higher note. *"Ai yi yi yi yi yiiiii!"* The fangers blinked and inched toward me. I held out my shovel and spun in a circle like a giant fidget spinner, whamming each one on the tip of the nose. They screamed and backed away, but did not run off like the other fanger had.

The shovel and my high note hadn't scared them. What else did I have?

A hammer. I yanked it out of my pocket. If I threw it once, that was it. And I didn't want to get close enough to whack them with it. Its handle was way shorter than the shovel's.

"Come and get me!" I said, my voice wobbling. I backed away slowly, and the fangers stalked after me, heads low. It was terrifying how they paced toward me, step by step. Deliberate. Fearless.

When I got to the edge of the tree well, I peered down. "Yarp?" I leaned in, trying to see any sign of him in the deep snow. Yarp wasn't there, but there was a mess of snow and dirt scattered everywhere. Near the bottom of the tree well was a small dark hole. Freshly dug.

"Come and get me!" I called to the fangers, and then I turned my back on them, something you should never, ever do to a large, hungry cat. I quickly jumped feet first into the deep tree well.

Four snarling heads leaned down, so close their foul breath was warm on my face. I gripped my

hammer tightly and whacked the tree trunk as hard as I could. The whole tree shuddered. I smashed it again. An avalanche of snow let loose from every branch of the tree, which reached about a hundred feet into the sky. The fangers shrieked, and I dove for the spot where I'd seen the small hole. The fangers were tumbling into the tree well, about to land on top of me, when I fell through the hole and into a narrow tunnel.

Yarp hadn't been able to climb out of the tree well. So he had dug *down*. Now the roof of the tunnel shook with the fangers scrambling to try to escape. Piles of snow were falling on them, blinding them in a white whirlwind.

I elbowed my way down the tight, dark tunnel. A streak of fear gripped my heart. *It's too tight— you'll get stuck.* You're the best digger in the whole school! some other part of me answered. *But I don't know where I'm going.* That's never stopped you before! *And it's dark.* The dark is your friend! The dark is your friend!

Elbow, elbow, knee, knee, I crawled through the tunnel. Elbow, elbow, knee, knee, and the smell of earth was all around me. I could see brown. The dirt walls crumbled, and I fell through the air, crash-landing right in the middle of the yarpies' den.

It was empty. No Yarp. I hoped he had gotten away with the rest of his family.

I threw on my backpack, grabbed my sled and climbed out of the den. The clearing was empty, and there were no yarpies or fangers in sight, though there were pine needles and chunks of white and brown fur everywhere.

I zigzagged along the trail through the trees. I spotted the big yarpie who'd been attacked by the four fangers, leaning against a fallen log. It didn't look like it was doing so great. I went and stroked its neck. Behind it I spotted Yarp, growling into the forest.

"Yarp!"

He spun around and bounded over to me. The big yarpie gave Yarp a long lick on top of his head. I knew it had to be Yarp's mom.

"Can you get up?" I looked her over. There were slash marks all over her back, but none of them looked too deep.

I tugged on Mama Yarp's front paw. She rolled over and with a terrible roar stood up. One of her hind legs dangled uselessly and had a bloody gash on it. She hopped on three legs for a short distance and then lay down, panting, against another snow-covered fallen log. I had to get her out of this place to somewhere safer. The den? And where had the rest of the yarpies gone? I was sure at least one of the fangers would return soon.

Yarp whined and turned back the other way, facing into the forest. He growled. A hiss came from the trees. I could see them now, at least three fangers, hanging back, eyeing us. Three of us and three of them. We'd make a pretty good lunch.

I drew my sled alongside Mama Yarp, then tugged at her paw. "Get up, get up! Get on the sled!" I pointed at the sled, but she didn't move. I threw myself on it to demonstrate.

Yarp barked. The fangers were slinking closer.

"Get up!" I screamed. I threw my arms around her front leg and heaved. She grunted but barely shifted. I skidded around to the other side of her and shoved my arms under her shoulder. My hands grasped two huge tufts of her fur, and I pulled with all I had.

Mama Yarp roared and rose on three legs. I leaned back, planted my foot on her shoulder and lifted her as best I could. She crashed down onto the sled, landing right in the middle.

The fangers were one pounce away. Yarp held them off, dodging left and right at dizzying speed, a yarping firestorm of short, sharp teeth.

I leaned my back against Mama Yarp's backside and shoved. The sled moved easily on the icy trails the yarpies had packed down. Spinning around, I thrust my palms against her furry haunches and pushed. The sled picked up speed and was soon racing down the hill. I wouldn't be able to keep up any longer, so I grabbed Mama Yarp's thick fur and leapt on top of her.

I looked over my shoulder. Yarp was running full tilt behind us, with the fangers slashing at his heels. Hanging on to Mama Yarp's fur, I flipped myself around so I was riding backward.

The fangers were bounding closer. "Yarp!" I screamed. "Jump!" I leaned out over the back of Mama Yarp and held out my arms. One of the fangers chomped down on Yarp's behind. He howled and threw himself at me. I grabbed his two paws. His back legs were dragging in the snow. With a massive heave, I hauled him up. The fanger running behind us spat out a chunk of white fur from Yarp's haunch. I buried my face in Mama Yarp's furry back and held on tight.

TWENTY-ONE

We flew down the hill. Every time I braced to go one way, the sled curved in the opposite direction. Yarp inched toward me until our noses were almost touching. It felt like the ride down the icy trail was never going to end. Had we started at the top of a mountain? Eventually our sled slowed. I took a deep breath, and then my heart did a double backflip as we launched off a bank and into the air.

We sailed through space for a second and then landed with a great *shoof* in soft snow. All was quiet. All was still. I raised my head. Yarp did too. We were now nose-to-nose. I heard soft snuffling noises coming closer. Yarp growled, and then his mom growled too. It was like sitting on top of an engine.

I was thinking about grabbing a tree branch to whack the fangers with when the rest of Yarp's clan peered over the edge of the bank. Yarp clicked his tongue and scrambled up the steep bank. He ran from one yarpie to the next, bumping them with his snout, before doing a somersault back down the bank. He grabbed the sled's rope in his teeth and tried to pull his mom back up, but he didn't have the strength.

Two of the other yarpies slid down. They grabbed the rope and started to pull.

"Wait!" I cried. "One of you has got to push, or Yarp's mom is just going to roll off the sled." I jumped down and pushed her backside. "See?"

All the yarpies were staring at me. Yarp joined me and began to push too. Finally one of the other yarpies waded through the snow to help us. Together the four of us pushed and pulled Yarp's injured mom up the bank on the sled. At the top Yarp sniffed her face and gave her a lick on the nose. She opened her eyes and gave him a super-lick right between his furry ears.

Yarp grabbed my coat sleeve and dragged me around to his mom's back leg. The gash was oozing blood. Yarp let go of my arm and sniffed the wound. He looked at me. Then back at the gash.

"It's a lot bigger than the cut you had," I said.

Yarp trotted over to the sled and returned with my backpack. What was I going to do? I wasn't sure if I had a bandage big enough. The yarpies had all sat down, and they watched me patiently, as though they were sure I could save their friend.

I thought of what I'd learned researching how to help Yarp.

I needed a clean cloth to press on the wound to stop the bleeding. But I didn't have a cloth. *Oh, wait!* I dug my pajama top out of my bag.

Once the bleeding stopped, I would have to bandage the wound. I held one palm against my pajama top and used my other hand to fish in the backpack. I pulled out a rolled-up tensor bandage.

But she'll just eat it, I thought. Then again, maybe Mama Yarp didn't have as weird an appetite as her son did. I had to let go of the top to start wrapping, but I hoped the wound had stopped bleeding. I looped the bandage around her leg, tight but not too tight.

It took some time, as I had to wiggle my hand and the bandage under her furry thigh and to the other side.

"Yarp," I said quietly. His ears pricked. "Do you think those fangers are going to come after us?"

He growled.

"We can't stay here." I looped the bandage around and around, trying to work as fast as I could. "They'll shred us to pieces." When I finally drew around the last bit of bandage, I carefully pinned down the end, trying not to poke Mama Yarp. "We've got to go back to my house."

Yarp tilted his head. I kept talking. "I know—there's no room for all of you." I had to think!

And that's when I came up with my mind-blowing idea.

"You guys can stay at the school! The kids have already built a whole bunch of tunnels right under the field."

Yarp sat down. Did he understand anything I'd said? I tried to tell the story with my hands, making signs for tunnels and diggers and the school. "I know the tunnels aren't large enough right now, but we can easily make them bigger. You guys are awesome diggers, and I know my way around the school. You can stay there until your mom can walk again."

I glanced over at his mother. Her eyes were closed. I hoped she was sleeping.

"She needs to rest in a safe place. Like you did, Yarp. I promise I'll take care of her."

Yarp stood up and shook his body hard. Snowflakes and white hair flew into the air. Yarp ambled from yarpie to yarpie. He touched whiskers with each of them and blew lightly into their nostrils. It seemed like he was communicating with them, although I had no idea what he was saying.

While I waited, I thought about what it would be like to see everyone again. Mom would probably freak out, even though I had left a note for her. All the kids would be mad at me. Especially Captain Frances and Spooky. They probably thought I was a traitor to both the Packrats and the Weasels. Everybody would hate me.

Yarp came back and tugged my sleeve with his teeth. He walked off into the forest, and I stumbled after him. "Look, we can't leave your family here,"

I said, turning around. "They have to come with us." I was worried he hadn't understood me at all.

One of the largest yarpies stood up and took the sled rope in his mouth. He pulled Mama Yarp toward us. Another yarpie lowered its head and pushed her haunch. The rest of the creatures stepped in behind, the snow crunching under their wide, flat paws.

Our walk through the forest was exhausting. The snow was deep, and there was no trail that I could see. The first time Yarp had brought me this way, I'd been asleep or conked out. I didn't recognize anything. At least he seemed to know where he was going. Even though I walked in Yarp's footprints, my legs grew heavy with the effort. At one point Yarp stopped and stared at something off to

the side. I pulled up behind him. There was a large mound covered in snow, with some white, curved sticks poking out of it. The other yarpies caught up and paused too. They hung their heads and made deep lowing sounds. The sticks were curved and reminded me of something.

Bones.

I looked closer and I saw the bones of many creatures scattered across the clearing. I wondered if they were the rest of the yarpies' clan, who had been ambushed or killed by the fangers. Was that why the others looked like they were starving? Maybe they had been trapped in their cave and were being picked off one by one. Or maybe there weren't enough of them to fight the fangers. We stood there, not moving, until I sensed that the yarpies were ready to go. They all turned at once, and we walked off together through the forest. I felt like I belonged with them.

TWENTY-TWO

The more I thought about it, the more I believed school was the perfect place for the yarpies to camp out. The only problem was the students. Somehow I had to persuade them to hide the yarpies in the tunnels without telling any of the teachers or their parents. Could they keep the secret? I was pretty sure Captain Frances and Spooky could. They'd already built the forts and snowball arsenals and tunnels and kept it all under the radar. But what about Koko and Lucas? Maybe, maybe not. And Mattie and Jackson? They would use any excuse to get me in trouble. The more I thought about it, the more my idea seemed impossible. But if I didn't help the yarpies,

I was sure Mama Yarp would end up as fanger food, and maybe the rest of them would too.

I thought of what Captain Frances had said to me. *Anything is possible.* It was true—sometimes you didn't know what you could do until you'd done it. If I could get her and Spooky to help me, maybe they could convince everyone else to keep the secret. I just wasn't sure if they'd want to help me anymore.

Yarp led us out of the wilderness. We walked and walked and walked through the snow and forest. We couldn't stop. What if the fangers were following us? My legs were so tired. At least I was warm, and we were going downhill.

Suddenly Yarp stopped. He cocked his head. All the yarpies did the same. I cocked my head too. Nothing. Yarp took off again at a faster pace. After a couple of minutes I heard it. Highway traffic. We had finally reached the road. And the snowbank tunnels.

We waited for dark. When the road grew quiet, one of the bigger yarpies dove into the snowbank and dug into the tunnel inside, using his great paws. Snow and ice flew at us. As soon as there was a large enough opening, the rest of us climbed in.

It was a lot easier walking in the tunnel after the trek through the forest. The snow was packed down.

There were no fallen logs to climb over or tree branches to dodge. The big yarpies barely fit into the tunnel, but they seemed happy enough to travel along in the dark. I could hear their soft grunts and padded paws stepping behind us, and the shush of the sled sliding along the snow.

It seemed like we'd hiked an ultra marathon when suddenly my legs went from feeling mostly dead to like they were burning up in flames. The tunnel was going uphill now, and I knew that meant we were not far from my school and home. Before long we reached two sharp bends in the snowbank.

"Help me get out, Yarp."

Together we dug an exit and popped out at the end of the school field. I was right.

"Yarp," I said, motioning to the field, "we should dig a tunnel and some dens under the school field for you to hide in." I grabbed my shovel and started digging down.

Yarp dug next to me, his large paws furiously scooping the snow away from the hole. One of the yarpies stepped out and looked around. He joined Yarp in his digging. And then the strangest and most amazing thing happened. All the other yarpies followed, like a train of yarpie boxcars.

The snow flew out of the tunnel. Each of them shuffled the snow backward, out of the hole and onto the edge of the field, where they spread it around or stamped it down to stop the snow from building up into a pile. When the snow finally stopped flying out, I popped on my headlamp and followed the last yarpie inside. I didn't have far to go before I reached a series of small dens they had just built.

Yarp was tucked in next to his mom, who lay dozing on the sled. I curled up against Yarp and ate my last pepperoni stick. He kept snuffling my neck, so I gave him half, which of course he swallowed in one gulp. Then I told him about my plan. The next morning at recess I would go and ask the kids for help. We needed them to watch over the yarpies and give them food from their lunches. One of the yarpies lay down beside us, and when Yarp climbed on top, I did too. It was a lot better sleeping on a furry, heated yarpie mattress than on a block of ice.

The school bell woke me up. Yarp and I scarfed down a granola bar and then we dug another tunnel that came out right inside the Packrat fort. I wrote a note, folded it in half and put Captain Frances's name on the outside. Then I left it at the entrance of the tunnel.

For Captin Franses Eyes Only:

I need your help. I am hiding in the tunnels. I also have a big surprise for you. Dont worry it's not a bad one.

Sinseerly, Lutenant Digger

We waited for recess. Finally the bell rang, and we heard the whumping sounds of kids running around above us. There was a hush. Arguing voices. A scraping noise in the hole. It was Captain Frances coming down. She stared at me, her eyes round. She spoke in a rush. "Henry, the whole world's been looking for you! Have you been down in this hole the whole time?"

"No."

"Your mom's really upset, and the police came to our school, and everybody's been all over town searching for you." She took a quick breath. "Where were you?"

"On an adventure."

Captain Frances sniffed and gave me a hard stare. "Well, you should have told someone, Lieutenant Digger."

"I left a note."

"Right," she said, squinting in the gray light. "I got the note you left for me. You said you needed my help."

"I do."

"I think you should tell your mom you're okay first."

"After. There's something you have to see."

"What?"

"Just come with me."

"How can I trust you, Henry? You said you would be a spy for the Packrats, and you double-crossed us," she whispered in a fierce growl.

Oh no. She knew.

She stared at me again. "When you disappeared, the police talked to a whole bunch of us kids. After that Spooky told me you were spying on the Packrats. That you were going to tell the Weasels where all our tunnels were. And how big our snow-ball stockpile was. That's not cool, Henry. Why did you do that?"

I squirmed inside, wishing I could be back with Yarp, where things were less complicated, where words didn't get me into so much trouble. "I guess I wanted Spooky and the other kids to like me."

"But I *already* liked you."

She looked confused, hurt, the way I had felt all those times the other kids had been mean to me. It was time to admit the truth. "I wanted *everyone* to like me."

"It's not nice when someone lies to you, Henry. It's like they think you're stupid. It's like they don't care about you."

"I'm sorry. I really do care about you."

"Then you have to be honest with your friends."

"I was at first," I said. I thought about how I had told Koko and Lucas about the Thing, and they hadn't believed me. "And then it all got mixed up. My friends called me a liar. And then I turned into a liar. After that I thought maybe telling a few lies could fix things. But it just got worse."

"Yeah. It did."

I felt terrible.

"You're telling the truth right now, though, aren't you?"

"Yes."

Captain Frances smiled. "Good. So just keep going."

Maybe she was right. I could carry on with the truth and get a do-over. A fresh-snow day. A clean start.

"So are you going to come out? If not, I have to tell Mrs. Zink you're hiding in the tunnel." Captain Frances started to crawl backward.

"Wait!" I cried. "Yarp?"

"Yarp?" said Yarp, shuffling up behind me.

Captain Frances froze.

Yarp's short snout and long whiskers poked over my shoulder. His warm breath blew into my ear.

"This is Yarp. He's here with his family, and they need our help."

Captain Frances just stood there, her mouth hanging open.

"See, I was telling the truth about some things." I grinned. "Didn't you believe me?"

"I did…" She gulped. "But sometimes even when you're looking right at it, the truth can be hard to believe."

Captain Frances followed us back to one of the dens, and I introduced her to Yarp's mom. She gently reached out to stroke Mama Yarp on the neck. "We're going to do what we can to help you out, Mama."

Yarp's mom groaned. She sounded sad.

"Don't worry, Mama Yarp," I said. "You're going to be okay." I didn't know if it was true, but I really hoped it would be. A thick lump grew in my throat as I thought of my own mom. I missed her so much, and all I wanted was one of her python power hugs.

I took Captain Frances's hand and led her back into the tunnel where Yarp was already waiting.

"They're incredible," she whispered in awe. "Like giant polar bears, but different. How many yarpies are there?"

"Fifteen," I said. "And they all need food. Do you think you can get some from the kids?"

"Of course. But will it be enough? How long are they going to stay?"

"A couple of weeks? Until Yarp's mom can walk again."

Captain Frances rubbed her forehead. "I'm worried the kids won't be able to keep it a secret for that long, Lieutenant. They're not exactly known for their discipline."

"But if we don't help the yarpies, the fangers will kill them."

"The *what*?"

"They're these giant cats with huge teeth that live in the deep forest. Like saber-toothed tigers. I think the reason the yarpies are all so thin is the fangers had them trapped in a hidden valley. They were picking them off one by one, and they had killed a whole lot of them at some point. When we tried to escape, Mama Yarp got hurt."

"I'll do my best, Lieutenant," Captain Frances said, giving me a curt nod.

"There's one more thing. The fangers might be following us."

She blinked. "How many fangers?"

"Three at least. Maybe more."

"*Maybe* more?"

"I don't know how many managed to escape from the tree well."

"Right. You can fill me in on the details later." She was silent for a few moments, staring through me. Then her eyes focused, and she gave me her fierce captain's gaze. "Okay, I have a plan. But it's going to take a lot of hard work. And you have to go home, Lieutenant."

"I'm staying here with Yarp."

"You want my tactical genius? Go home to your mom. That's an order."

TWENTY-THREE

"Hey, Mom, I'm home!" I yelled as I walked into the mudroom.

Mom came stumbling around the corner from the kitchen and burst into tears. She hugged me hard. While I'd been away, her python-strength squeeze had upgraded to a crocodile death roll.

"I missed you, Mom."

"I missed you too, Henry," she choked out. "I'm so glad you're all right." She finally released me from the crocodile hug and looked me up and down, still hanging on to my arms. "Where were you?"

"I went to live in the woods."

She wiped her cheeks. "With Bart Yarp?"

"Um, yeah."

"Henry. I know he's an imaginary friend. And you made him up because the other kids are mean to you."

"Sort of." After all, she was half-right. I didn't know a person or creature named Bart Yarp. "But I'm not worried about the other kids now, Mom. Captain Frances is still my friend."

"Are you sure?"

"Yeah."

"You're not going to run away again, are you?"

"Nope. It was rough living without you."

She burst out laughing and squeezed me some more. "But where did you sleep?"

"In a cave."

Mom leaned back, and her face clouded over. "Where?"

"In the woods."

"It's a miracle you didn't freeze to death," she said. "But I have a feeling you're not telling me the whole story."

I didn't say anything. I didn't know where to start. I hoped that one day I could tell her everything.

"Just promise me you won't do it again."

"I promise."

Mom contacted the police and the school and told them I was back safe and sound. Then she took me to the hospital for a checkup. I told Dr. Fluff I'd had no more concussion symptoms. No headaches, no dizziness. She said I was in perfect shape and could return to regular activity. Slowly. I didn't tell her it was a little late for that.

On our way out, an ambulance pulled into the emergency bay. The back doors swung open and Bart the Mustache jumped out.

"Hey! Hi!" I waved my hand in the air like crazy.

He looked over my way in surprise. "Oh hey, kid, how're you doing?"

"Good! I saw a Thing."

"You saw a Thing?" he asked, pulling a stretcher out of the ambulance.

"With tons of hair!"

He wheeled a person in ski gear past us, and his mustache smiled. "I knew you would." They disappeared through the sliding doors.

"What was that all about?" Mom asked.

"Ah, nothing, just a story he told me."

But in my head I heard Bart the Mustache singing the last lines of his song. *And in the woods I saw a Thing with tons of hair, my heart went zing!*

We crossed the parking lot and found our car under an inch of snow. "Hey, Mom, can we go to the grocery store and get a mango?"

"Did you say a mango? They're not exactly in season right now."

"I'm really craving a mango."

Mom brushed the snow off the top of her door. "A mango. You must be missing some essential vitamin in your diet. But okay."

The next day Mom drove me to school and dropped me off, giving the don't-mess-with-my-kid stare to every kid walking to school.

Mrs. Zink played it cool, smiling at me as if I'd just been on a short holiday. "It's so lovely to have you back, Henry."

All the kids were super nice during class, but I wondered if that would last beyond the first recess bell. They were all staring at me and trying not to at the same time. It was creeping me out. Once again I was the weirdo, the one who didn't fit in. As we were getting ready for recess, I noticed that all the kids were quietly stuffing their coat pockets with food. Oranges, bananas, cookies, sandwiches and plastic containers filled with mystery snacks.

The kids ran out onto the playground, yelling their heads off just like usual. It was snowing heavily, so hard you could barely see the fence at the end of the field. Nothing appeared strange at all. I decided to take a risk, hoping Captain Frances would stand up for me, and headed over to the Packrat fort.

Inside, hidden from the rest of the school, was the tunnel entrance. Kids were running into the fort, emptying their pockets of food into a bag held by Lucas and then running out again. They called things like, "Hi, Henry!" and "We've got your back, Henry!"

To my amazement, Koko popped out of the tunnel entrance with an empty bag in her hands. She took Lucas's place collecting the recess snacks from the kids, and Lucas entered the tunnel with the full bag.

"Are you giving them food?" I asked.

"Yeah. They're really hungry." She grinned. "You should see them gobble it all down."

I felt a rush of happiness, thinking about the starving yarpies finally getting some food other than dry lichen.

"So…Henry?" said Koko, shyly.

"Yeah?"

Just then a small boy from the third grade, with a pom-pom on his toque, appeared in the doorway of the fort. Koko held out her empty cloth bag, and the boy dropped a bag of carrots and celery in, watching it fall to the bottom.

"Can I see them?" he asked.

"Shhh," Koko said. "It's top secret. Don't even talk about them. Maybe if you get me some more food from your class, I'll take you down there."

The boy ran out of the fort, and the two of us were alone.

I opened up my backpack and threw my sandwich and orange into Koko's bag. The golden yellow mango sat at the bottom of my pack, perfectly ripe.

"This is for you," I said, pulling it out and handing it to Koko. "They're the best fruit in the whole world."

"I know what a mango is, Henry." She took the mango in her mitt.

"I'm sorry I got you in trouble, Koko. I shouldn't have asked you to go off the school grounds. I never wanted you to get a detention."

"You were right—it wasn't a big deal."

"What did you have to do?"

"Principal Kirkland asked me and Lucas what our favorite songs were. Then he looked them up on YouTube. After we listened to them, we had to write new lyrics for one verse."

"Oh yeah." I nodded. "I've done that detention before. Took *forever*."

"And when we were done, he got out his guitar, and we all sang the new verses. He said he thought my lyrics were better than the original."

"Well, that's cool, 'cause he never said that about mine. I'd like to hear them sometime."

"Okay." Koko glanced down the tunnel. "I'm sorry I didn't believe you about the tunnels, Henry. And the yarpies."

"It's all good," I said, and it was.

Lucas climbed out of the tunnel hole with his empty bag and switched places with Koko.

"Can you hang on to this for me?" she asked and handed the mango back to me. "We can share it later." Koko slipped down into the tunnel and disappeared.

Lucas grinned at me. "Hey, Henry." He paused. "I think the little yarpie likes me."

I knew that was how Lucas was saying he was sorry too.

"Which little yarpie?" I said with a tiny twinge of jealousy pinging in my heart. Yarp was *my* buddy. "Does he have some fur missing on his leg?"

"No, I don't think so. He's white with blue eyes."

"Oh, that one. He's really nice." I felt a flood of relief. They were all white with blue eyes, but if the young yarpie Lucas had made friends with didn't have a patch of fur missing, it wasn't Yarp. I really needed the kids' help, but I wasn't ready to share my buddy, not yet.

"I'm glad you came back, Henry. This is the coolest thing that's ever happened here."

"Thanks, Lucas," I said. "And thanks for helping."

"Captain Frances wanted me to tell you when you got here that you should go to the Weasel fort."

I crossed the field in the snowstorm, watching the kids, who seemed to already know how to enter the Packrat fort in ones and twos to drop off their food so they wouldn't catch the supervisor's attention. More than anything, I wanted to see the yarpies eating the recess snacks, but I didn't dare mess up Captain Frances's plan.

I took a deep breath before stepping inside the Weasel fort. If Captain Frances thought I was a double-crosser, did Spooky think I was a triple-crosser? Or was that a double-double-crosser? Telling all the lies had made my head spin, just like the concussion had. Once you started, they piled on top of each other until you couldn't keep track. You could get crushed under the weight of them.

Captain Frances was drawing black lines with an erasable marker on a mini whiteboard with Spooky and a few others gathered around her.

"Lieutenant Digger, good, you're here," said Captain Frances. "We need your opinion. We've never seen these fangers before, so you're going to have to give us some intel."

That was weird. No one had ever asked me for my opinion before. And even weirder, Captain Frances and Spooky seemed to have joined forces. Were the Weasels and Packrats no longer at war?

Spooky stepped aside to make a gap for me in the circle. They all turned back to the whiteboard, and I realized the black squiggles and squares were the tunnels and forts of the Packrats and Weasels.

"This is what we're going to do," said Captain Frances, after I'd told them all I knew about the fangers. "We'll dig a tunnel connecting the Weasel fort to the roadside tunnel. There's already a skinny tunnel that goes halfway there. We'll build up our snowball ammo, and when the fangers get here, we let 'em have it."

She was talking about the tunnel I had built, which was supposed to be a Weasel secret. I put up my hand. "Permission to speak?"

"Granted," said Captain Frances.

"Are the Weasels and Packrats…ah…getting along now?" I asked.

Spooky and Captain Frances looked at each other. "Yes," they both said.

"We have a common enemy," said Captain Frances.

"Oh, well, good." I looked back at the whiteboard and pointed at a thick line. "I'm worried about the tunnel that goes from the main road to the Packrat fort. It goes right past the yarpies' den. Yarp's mom can't defend herself while she's injured."

Spooky took the marker from Captain Frances. "We could close up this access to the yarpies," he said, drawing a line across the entrance to the yarpies' den.

"But then how are we going to get food to them?" said Captain Frances.

I stared hard at the whiteboard. "We'll have to dig another tunnel from their den to the Packrat fort," I said.

"Roger that," said Captain Frances. "So there'll be a tunnel from the roadside to the Packrat fort, to the Weasel fort and back out to the roadside tunnel. Like a big loop. And one more from the Packrat fort to the yarpie den."

"It's not good enough," said Spooky, shaking his head. "You said these fangers are huge. What if they're not scared off?"

He was right. I had been pummeled by at least a hundred snowballs and managed to get on my feet afterward. Snowballs alone wouldn't stop the fangers.

"What if they attack us?" Spooky added. "Snatch up some little kid?"

"That'd be bad," I agreed. I guess it hadn't occurred to him that he could get eaten too. Or else he was really brave.

"And how do we know they'll even stick to the tunnels? What if they come across the snow field?"

"They don't like being out in the open," I said. "They like the forest. And the tunnels. I think that's why no one has ever seen the yarpies and the fangers before. Until this year."

"Why now?" asked Captain Frances.

"I think it's because there's so much snow this year. The snowbanks are huge. Maybe they never had a chance to leave their secret valleys before."

"Right." Captain Frances grabbed the marker and began making big X's and more squiggles on the whiteboard. "We need to control the tunnels and the forts and use them to our advantage. Really scare them."

"How do we do that?" asked Spooky.

We stared at the smears on the whiteboard. Thinking about how we were going to get out of this mess hurt my head, and I then remembered how it all had started—when I got squashed after Jackson and Mattie jumped on the first tunnel I dug.

"What if we used one of the *big* snowballs to crush the fangers? The ones the Weasels make."

"Who's going to throw it?" asked Spooky. "A giant?"

"We roll it over the top of one of the tunnels, and it falls through and squashes them."

Spooky looked confused. "How's it going to fall through?"

Captain Frances drew a line across the whiteboard. She sketched a dip in the line and next to it, on top of the line, a big Weasel snowball. "We dig down on top of the tunnel in one spot, until the roof of the tunnel is thinner there than on the rest of the field. And then we push the big snowball onto it."

"There's only one problem," I said. "How are we going to figure out exactly where the tunnels are?"

Captain Frances smiled. "My dad trained me how to search for someone who's caught in an avalanche. We can use his beacons and a probe."

Spooky brushed at the snow on the whiteboard, and the map was smeared into a streaky mess. "It'll still take us forever to dig those tunnels. We've only got seven shovels. Eight, counting Henry's. And most of the kids can't dig their way through a bowl of ice cream, let alone a tunnel."

"Actually, we've got fifteen of the best diggers on the planet," I said. "Fourteen, not counting Yarp's mom."

"How do we know you can get them to do it?" asked Spooky.

"They trust me," I said.

"Okay." Spooky looked at me carefully. "But how do we know we can trust *you*?"

I didn't know how to prove that. Words were all I had, and they had gotten me into so much trouble. "I'm sorry I wasn't telling the truth before. I'm doing my best to fix that."

Spooky held out his mitt, and I stared at it, not knowing what to do. "Shake," he said, and we did.

"Good. We're all one unit," said Captain Frances. "Spooky, you start work on the Weasel territory. I'll organize the Packrats and bring my gear tomorrow, and Henry can get the yarpies to support the mission."

Spooky saluted Captain Frances, and I did the same. We stepped out of the Weasel fort into the wind and gusts of blowing snow.

TWENTY-FOUR

With the help of the yarpies, the changes to the tunnels took only two recesses and one lunch hour to build. I started digging where we wanted to go. And then, after some whisker waggling and nostril blowing between them, Yarp and the yarpie digging train took the lead.

Captain Frances taught Jackson and Mattie how to use the avalanche beacons and probe. After that Mattie and Koko went into the tunnel that led from the road to the Packrat fort. They used one of the beacons and set the signal to transmit.

Meanwhile, in the middle of the school field, Jackson and I switched the other beacon to receive. Together we tramped around in the snow until

the beacon showed us we were above Mattie and Koko in the tunnel. I pulled Frances's probe out of my backpack. It was like five sticks that snapped together into one really long stick. I poked the probe into the snow until it wiggled, which meant Mattie and Koko were shaking the end of it.

Then they joined us up top. Koko and I dug a large dip above the tunnel while Jackson and Mattie rolled a snowball around the field. The snowball grew so big it took all four of us to roll it into place right next to the big dip. Ready to be launched. The next day we did the same thing on the other side of the field, above the tunnel that went from the Weasel fort back to the road.

After that we waited. Everyone was tense, not knowing if, or when, the fangers would turn up. Captain Frances barked at the Packrats to make more snowballs. Spooky marched around reminding all the kids not to tell anyone about the yarpies and asking them to bring more food from home.

The good news was that with each day that went by, Mama Yarp's wounds healed a little more, and the yarpies looked healthier. They gained weight, and their white coats grew thicker. All the kids were laughing secretly about how happy their parents were when they brought home empty lunch boxes every day. I was scared, though, that sooner or later someone would let our secret slip.

I felt like I was holding my breath the whole time. Still, I had a whole bunch of friends now, real friends who were okay with me being a little weird. Every day we played with Yarp and his buddies, making up funny games like Seek the Snack and Leap-Yarpie. But I knew it wasn't going to last much longer. When Yarp's mom got better, they would have to leave and find a new secret valley, far away from the fangers. I wondered if I would ever see Yarp again.

If we didn't have as much snow next winter, maybe they wouldn't be able to dig tunnels inside the snowbanks, and travel unseen by the rest of the world. Then again, if it really was the beginning of an ice age, perhaps there would be even more snow next winter. I couldn't help smiling at the possibility.

Then one day at recess, as we were chasing through the tunnels having a great game of Find the Furball, I heard the muffled shout of a familiar voice.

"Breach, breach!" screamed Koko.

The Packrat fort was under attack! I sprinted out of Yarp's den, my headlamp lighting my way up the tunnel. I popped out inside the fort, near the entrance. On the other side of the fort, only a couple of feet away, a fanger's head poked out of the tunnel that led to the roadside. It snarled at the Packrats, and they threw a hundred snowballs down on the beast. Behind it, two other fangers yowled, trying to squeeze out of the tunnel.

"Battle stations!" shouted Captain Frances from the top of the fort wall. I climbed up to join her and a line of Packrats, including Koko and Lucas. There was no time to be scared. We pelted the fangers with iceballs.

Smash! Thud! We nailed them with direct hits to the nose. The fangers wailed and retreated into the tunnel. Would they return to the road or continue along the tunnel to the Weasel fort? Our plan was to squash them on their way in and scare them off, but they had already made it to the Packrat fort.

Captain Frances waved a shovel high in the air and shouted across the field. "Mattie! Jackson! They're coming!"

On the far side of the field, Mattie and Jackson ran over to the first giant snowball.

"Now!" shouted Captain Frances.

Mattie and Jackson pushed the snowball, but it didn't budge. Mattie whistled, and a few other kids ran over to help push. "One, two, three, shove!"

The snowball rolled into the dip in the field. Nothing. Mattie and Jackson climbed on top and jumped up and down. *Whoof!* The giant snowball disappeared, dropping down through the surface of the snow into the tunnel. Muffled shrieks and yowls erupted from the hole. A second passed. Mattie and Jackson climbed back up and fist-pumped the air. The Packrats let out a big cheer.

But where were the fangers now? Had they escaped to the road? Been completely squashed? Or had the snowball cut them off, and now they were on their way back to the Packrat fort?

"Reload, Packrats!" cried Captain Frances. Every kid on the wall leaned down to the shelves and grabbed as many iceballs as they could hold.

Captain Frances pumped her shovel in the air and shouted across the field. "Weasels! Get to your battle stations!"

We waited for a sign from the Weasels, but none came. Hadn't they heard her? The snow was falling in thick clumps, muffling everything. Where were they?

Captain Frances pointed at me. "Henry, go! Warn the Weasels. We have to be prepared for anything!"

I leapt down from the wall and thrashed through the heavy snow.

On my way to the Weasel fort, I hoped Ms. Shear hadn't noticed all the ruckus. We'd told the kindies to distract her. To stomp on each other's snow angels and do some fake crying. It was all part of the plan for supervisor distraction, and they were putting on an award-worthy performance. I saw one kid rolling around in agony. But how long would it work? I knew Ms. Shear couldn't see the fangers from where she stood, but she could definitely see the banned iceballs being chucked.

I kept running toward the Weasel fort and burst through the entrance, expecting to see them making iceballs or fixing up the walls. The fort was empty. Where were they? I stuck my head out of the entrance and scanned the field and schoolyard, searching for a tall, white-haired ghost boy. Spooky was nowhere to be seen, nor were any of the other Weasels.

Fear ripped through my guts. They had to be in the tunnels somewhere. With the fangers. I jumped down the hole at the back of their fort and into the tunnel. One way led back to the Packrat fort, and the other led to the only open route to the road. I had to warn the Weasels, but I didn't know which way to go. I turned toward the road.

"The fangers are coming!" I yelled. Had they heard? The snow walls smothered the sound. There was no way to run the length of the tunnel and get back in time before the fangers arrived. So I screamed. My high-pitched scream. *"The fangers are coming!"*

Silence.

The only thing left to do was head back toward the Packrat fort. Either I'd run into the Weasels to give them a warning, or I'd run into the fangers and I'd be dead. Within twenty steps I heard the unmistakable yowls and screeches of the gigantic saber-toothed cats. The tunnel grew lighter.

The fangers were still being pelted by snowballs at the edge of the hole inside the Packrat fort. They looked frightened and in rough shape, with clumps of snow hanging from their fur. There were fewer snowballs hitting them now, and I realized the Packrats had used up their stockpile and were making and throwing them as fast as they could.

"Hey, fangers!" I shouted. The first one whipped its head around and got an iceball to the ear. "Ya, ya, you can't get me!" Waving my arms wildly, I began to walk backward. The first fanger stalked toward me. Now I knew what a mouse feels like. I did something you should never do when you face a wild cat that is bigger than you. I turned and ran.

"The fangers are coming!" I shouted, hoping the Weasels had heard my first scream and returned to the fort. I heard the galloping sound of paws behind me. I expected two long, sharp teeth to dig into my neck any second.

I tripped. As I landed, I curled into a ball, wrapping my arms around my head and neck.

A vicious roar erupted. I prepared for death. The fangers ran right over top of me.

What the heck?

But then hot breath blew on my neck. Whiskers tickled my scalp. I rolled over and got a big lick up the side of my face from Yarp. He huffed once and then chased after the fangers. Two more yarpies followed, galloping over me. Once they'd passed, I leapt up and raced after them.

I reached the Weasel fort and climbed out of the tunnel.

"Hold your fire! It's Henry!" shouted Spooky. The Weasels stood on the fort walls, arms in the air, iceballs ready. Spooky called out to me. "The fangers and the yarpies have all run down toward the road. Do we squash them? Do we close the tunnel?"

"I don't know," I said. "What if we squash one of the yarpies? Or they get stuck on the other side with the fangers?"

"What do we do? We have to do something! The supervisor's coming over!"

I shut my eyes and tried to connect my thoughts to the yarpies. Where were they?

Nothing came. "Close it."

Spooky shouted across the field. "Mattie! Jackson! Release the snowball!"

I ran down the tunnel, hoping to catch up to the yarpies. I stopped, sensing the presence of a creature in front of me. Ahead, a huge *whumpf* nearly blew me over with an icy wind. The big snowball had fallen, blocking the tunnel.

Yarp walked out of a cloud of crystals. The other two yarpies ambled up behind him. He gave me a big wet lick, and I threw myself around him.

"Are the fangers gone?"

"*Yarp.*"

"We did it! We scared them off!"

I hoped the yarpies would have enough time now to find a new valley in the wilderness, someplace safe.

As we walked back toward the Weasel fort, I could hear the supervisor telling off the Weasels, her mitts clapping in time.

"You know *snow-balls-are-banned*. Every single one of you is *brea-king-that-rule*."

"Sorry," said Spooky.

"Why *would-you-do-that?*" asked the supervisor.

Spooky hesitated. "It was fun?"

"I don't see how hurting another person... what's *that*?"

"What's what?" he asked innocently.

"That hole." My heart nearly stopped. No doubt she was pointing to the hole that led to the tunnels.

I pushed on Yarp, forcing him and the other two yarpies backwards down the tunnel. I turned my headlamp off.

"Oh, the hole," said Spooky. "That's where we keep the snowballs."

Ms. Shear's voice grew louder. She was in the tunnel. "Hellooo?"

I held my breath.

"This is not a hole. This is a tunnel. And as you know, tunnels are also banned. They are extremely dangerous." Her voice faded. She was back in the fort. "I'll be telling Mr. Kirkland about this, and they'll have to be destroyed. Im-*me-di-ate-ly*." She finished with an extra-loud clap.

The bell rang, and I heard a lot of thuds from kids running overhead.

There was no time to say goodbye. I guess in my mind I had been saying goodbye to Yarp and his family for some time now, but it still hurt my heart now that the time for them to leave had come.

Although I didn't think the school would start filling in the tunnels that very same day, I was worried Mr. Kirkland would come down into the tunnels with his flashlight to investigate.

Since we'd blocked both entrances, the yarpie train had to dig through the first big snowball to get out of the labyrinth under the fields. Yarp's mom wasn't strong enough to dig, but she was able to walk now, and she took a spot in the middle of the train, where she was protected. We had to wait until school was out and the streets were quiet before they could cross the road. Yarp and I led them to the tunnel that ran past my house and in the opposite direction from the secret valley where they'd been held captive by the fangers.

We waited until the road was quiet, and then they dug their way out of the tunnel and made their way into the forest. Two yarpies hung back to help us close up the hole. When it was filled, Yarp leaned close to my face and waggled his whiskers. I hung on to his neck and buried my nose in his fur, breathing in the scent of moss and pine needes.

We turned to go at exactly the same time. He followed in the footprints of his clan, and I climbed to the top of the snowbank. I walked in the deep white snow back to the school, where my friends were waiting for me.

I thought about how lucky I was to have had a friend like Yarp, one who was there just when I needed him. And no matter how many friends I would have in the future, I knew I would never again have a best friend as furry and loyal as Yarp.

ACKNOWLEDGMENTS

It takes a village to write a book. My everlasting thanks goes to all the wonderful villagers who helped me build the world of this one:

My enduring, fabulous Vicious Circle—Katherine Fawcett, Stella Harvey, Sara Leach, Mary MacDonald, Libby McKeever and Sue Oakey-Baker, because our lives and stories grow together. All the terrific folks at Orca Book Publishers, especially Andrew Wooldridge, Rachel Page, Olivia Gutjahr and Vivian Sinclair. A special thank you to Tanya Trafford, my champion, for encouragement, insight and her open heart. To my incredible illustrator, Cornelia Li, who has truly captured the spirit of snow and wild creatures. Thank you to Caroline Adderson, who gave me exactly the right advice at exactly the right time. Huge gratitude to Grace Kary, whose excellent critique on structure had me cut the flab. For Maggie and Colin Wood, my mum and dad, who always encouraged me to go out and play in the forest. To my husband, James, for everything, and whose advice of "more explosions" is never far from my mind. And to Ollie and the cats, the greatest bedtime-story listeners ever.

REBECCA WOOD BARRETT is an award-winning writer and filmmaker whose short fiction has been published in literary journals such as *Room* and the *Antigonish Review*. She has an MFA in creative writing from the University of British Columbia and lives in Whistler, British Columbia, where she teaches writing and filmmaking to kids of all ages. For more information, visit rebeccawoodbarrett.com.